The Duck Springs Affair

By
John Isaac Jones

The Duck Springs Affair

A Winter Afternoon

It was early December of 2015. Along a lonely sidewalk, a middle-aged man pushed an elderly woman in a wheelchair across the grounds of an assisted care facility. The man was in shirtsleeves and the woman was wearing a heavy sweater and earmuffs with a thick blanket covering her legs and feet. In the dense thicket of Georgia pines and water oaks beyond them, the leafless trees stood cold and naked in their winter isolation.

"Mama," the man said. "Are you sure it's not too cold out here for you? I'm freezing."

"That's because you're not wearing a jacket, Paulie," the mother replied. "That little old thin shirt you got on won't hold any heat."

The son didn't answer at first.

"I guess you're right," he said finally. "I left my jacket in the car. I wish I had brought it. Where do you want me to park you?"

"Over there in front of that oak tree," the mother said, indicating with her head. "I can throw bread to the ducks without them getting out of the water."

Moments later, the man maneuvered the wheelchair off the sidewalk and onto the brown grass. As they approached the tree, she inspected the area around the base for the most comfortable spot.

"Try to stay away from those roots," she said. "I like for the wheelchair to be level."

The man moved the wheelchair to the designated spot.

"How's that?"

"Can you go a little further to the left?"

The man adjusted the position of the wheelchair.

"How's that?"

"That's fine," the mother said. "I'll be just fine right here."

The man peered across the winter lake. Already a flock of some two to three hundred ducks were bobbing up and down in the windswept water. In the distance, across the grey sky, he could see more ducks descending upon the lake.

"The ducks are coming in, Mama," he said. "They're waiting on you."

"I see 'em, baby," she replied.

Satisfied his mother was happily positioned, the man turned to say good-bye.

"Now, I won't be back for a couple hours," he said. "You've got your buzzer. You can call the nurse if you need something."

"I'll be fine," she said. "Go on and take care of your family. Don't worry about me."

"You're sure it's not too cold?" he asked. "And you brought plenty of bread for the ducks?"

"I'll be fine," she said again. "Just go on. I'll see you in a couple hours."

"Okay, Mama!" the man said. "I'm gone."

He took a few steps back down the sidewalk, then turned.

"I love you, Mama," he said.

"I love you too, baby," the mother replied.

* * * *

Every Saturday, my son Paulie comes to the old folks home where I live to visit me. On warm days, he likes to sit out on the veranda to talk and drink iced tea. On cold days, he always fusses when I tell him I want to get outside. He's afraid I'll catch a cold, but I know I'll be fine. When you get to be my age, cold don't bother like it does when you're young. I guess your skin just gets tougher as you grow older.

On winter afternoons like today, I like to come down to the lake to feed the ducks and be alone with my memories. Sometimes, I just have to get away from the home. I get tired of them treating me like a little child all the time. Do this! Do that! Time for your medicine! Bingo starts in ten minutes! Don't you want to watch TV? If it's not one thing, it's another. Everything is always so organized and cut-and-dried. I just need a break sometimes.

My name is Cassie Mae Carter and next spring, on March 16, 2016, I'll be eighty-one years old. My days are nearing their end, but I'm not afraid. I've seen the changing of the seasons and the movement from the old to the new for so long that I accept it without question. It all seems so natural. My life and the lives of all people are part of that constant ebb and flow. Birth and death are part of the natural order.

All I've ever been in my life was a simple country woman. All of my time has been spent close to the land and animals and crops. Taking care of a house, raising kids, milking the cow, shelling peas, churning butter, bringing in the stove wood, and making a garden every year is the story of my life. There are thousands of other women like me here in south Georgia. In fact, many of them are my friends here at the Golden Years Home.

For more than fifty years, I lived on a little farm near Duck Springs, Georgia. As the crow flies, it's about five miles from here. My husband Austin and I raised two boys, Timmy, a sickly child who always needed medical care, and Paulie, the handsome young man who wheeled me down to the lake today. He's fifty-three now and, from the day he was born, he has been the light of my life. Never could I have asked for a more wonderful, loving son. He's smart and good-hearted and devoted to his family. He has never run afoul of the law and, in times of trouble, he has always been there to love and comfort his mother.

The story you're about to hear has never been told. It has been a secret between me and my God for more than fifty years. It is a story that I fear to tell, yet I also know that it must be told before I leave this earth. This is the story of a love affair I had when I was a young woman. It is a story that has haunted me all my years. *Haunted?* you may ask. Although the affair brought me the most wonderful gift I ever owned, it also brought me a deep feeling of personal guilt that lives in my soul to this very day. This is the story of my son Paulie and how I became his mother.

New Job

April, 1961

Paul Hamilton, pulling one lever, then pushing another, expertly maneuvered the bulldozer up the hillside, its mighty engine belching black smoke and groaning under the strain of the uprooted Florida palmetto plants and pine saplings it was pushing with its front blade.

Clearing the vegetation between the road shoulders and the property right-of-way was the final phase of the Lake City, Florida project. Four months earlier, the concrete center slab and the bare shoulders for the new highway had been finished. Striping crews had painted the centerline and shoulder markings. Now all that remained was to erect a fence along the property right-of-ways to prevent animals from wandering out on the new highway. After that, grassing crews would shoot a mixture of tar, mulch, grass seed, and fertilizer across the road shoulders, which would create a carpet of lush green grass over the next few months. Then the new highway would be ready for traffic.

As he slowly backed the heavy machine down the hill for another pass, he saw a familiar pickup truck approaching down the finished center slab. The words "Gartman Highway Construction" were emblazoned on the driver's side door.

Paul watched as his foreman, Will Works, a tall, mustachioed man in his early fifties, got out and started walking toward him. As the foreman neared, he made an open-palmed up and down motion that indicated Paul should shut off the engine so they could talk. Paul pushed the ignition switch and the engine sputtered to a halt.

"What's up, boss?" Paul said.

"We'll be moving to the new job this weekend," Will said.

"Where we going?"

"Duck Springs, Georgia," Will replied. "Little town south of Albany."

"Another extension?"

"It's a widening project," Will said. "Going to make two lanes into four lanes. About a year's work."

"That's peach and pecan country," Paul said.

"And lots of cotton," Will added.

"So what's the plan?"

"Charley is taking two dozers and a grader up there and Pete is taking one of the pans," he said, referring to the giant earth-moving machines the company used to shave down hills and ridges. "I want you to take a lowboy and the other pan up there on Sunday."

"Sunday?" Paul said. "That's my day of rest."

"You'll get overtime," Will said. "We got to have all the equipment up there next week. Old man Gartman will have a fit if we don't get started by April 22."

"What about my pickup?" Paul asked.

"Knox will drive it up for you."

"I'll be ready," Paul said.

Will nodded his approval.

"Me and the boys are going to be down at Eddie's tonight," he said. "You want to join us?"

"I'll be there," Paul said.

"See you then," Will said.

Paul watched as Will turned and started walking back to the pickup. Will had been his boss for fourteen years, and during that entire time, Will had always treated him fairly and honestly. In some ways, Will had been more like a father to him than a boss. Once, when Paul got into a barroom fight in Nashville and was thrown in jail, Will bailed him out. Another time, Will had helped him overcome the death of his mother. Will had never had children of his own and, from time to time, he hinted that Paul was the son he had always wanted.

Moments later, Paul fired up the bulldozer again and started another pass back up the right-of-way. Inside, he felt a certain sadness at leaving Florida. Over the past year and a half, The Sunshine State had had its perks. He loved the warm weather, the tropical vegetation, and an occasional visit to the beach. No matter how cold it got, he never needed more than a light jacket. Best of all, his retired father lived in Ocala. If he wanted to visit his dad for a day, it was only three hours away. He would miss that.

* * * *

Eddie's Bar and Grill was a small roadside tavern/restaurant along Highway 117, which led into Lake City. Each time the Gartman crew took on a new project, they always managed to find a local watering hole where they could meet after work to eat, drink beer, and, for the single ones, meet women. Eddie's had been chosen for the Lake City job.

As Paul entered that night, his nose caught the smell of stale beer and cigarette smoke. In the corner, the jukebox was wailing a song of lost love, couples were dancing, and, along the wall toward the rear, several pool games were in progress. For a moment, Paul stopped and surveyed the crowd. Finally, his eyes fell on Will, Knox, Pete, and Charley at a table in the corner.

"Sit down," Will said.

"Let me get a beer and a pool table first," Paul said.

Quickly, he turned and headed toward the pool tables. As he strode across the barroom floor, Paul cut the figure of a handsome man. Tall, with wide, muscular shoulders and narrow hips, he moved with a gait that spoke of confidence and personal power. Here was a man any woman would be proud to have by her side. At the nearest pool table, he stopped, fished a quarter out of his pocket, then placed it on the rail for the next game. As he approached the bar, his eyes scanned the barstools for Brenda, his on-then-off-again lover. He didn't see her. As he waited for the bartender, another woman, a brunette dressed in blue jean cut-offs, a cowboy hat, and showing more than ample cleavage, tapped him on the shoulder. He turned.

"Hey, Paul," she said. "Want to buy me a drink?"

It was Janice, another regular he was occasionally paired with to play pool.

"Looks like you already had a few," he said.

"I can always use one more."

Paul smiled and turned to the bartender.

"One draft and a bloody Mary," he said.

Then he turned back to Janice.

"I see you're up for the next game," she said.

"Yeah," he said. "Want to play?"

"Sure."

Moments later, Paul and Janice were seated at the table with the Gartman crew. Janice, who was more than a bit tipsy, snuggled herself and her chair up close to Paul. As they chatted, she gently stroked his leg under the table. Suddenly, Paul looked across the room and saw Brenda approaching.

"Paul!" she called.

Paul looked up, then Brenda pulled back when she saw Janice.

For a moment, Brenda glared angrily at Janice. Then she turned to Paul.

"Who is this?" she asked.

"That's my friend Janice," Paul replied.

"With her hand on your leg like that, it looks like she's more than a friend."

"There's no need to get upset," Paul said.

"You don't like me anymore?"

"Look, Brenda," Paul said. "Don't start any trouble."

Brenda didn't hear a word he said.

Raging anger flashed across her face and, suddenly, in a furious rage, she was in Janice's face.

"Get away from him," she shouted, wagging her finger. "He belongs to me. You understand? He's mine!"

Janice, her face flushed with anger, stood up.

"Who in hell you think you're talking to?" she shouted.

For a moment, the two women glared angrily at one another.

"You hussy!" Brenda screamed. Then, in a fit of rage, she rushed toward the other woman. In a flurry of hair-pulling, face-scratching, screaming fury, the two women tumbled to the floor.

"Whoa! Whoa!" Will shouted, leaping from his chair.

For a moment, he circled the brawling women, then, seeing an opportunity, grabbed Janice's arms and pulled the women apart.

"Come on," Will said. "Cool off! Cool off!!"

Janice was standing now, breathing hard and glaring angrily at her adversary on the floor.

"You're nothing but a hussy," she shouted. "A low-life hussy. Do you hear me?"

At the words, Brenda leapt catlike to her feet and, in a new fit of rage, charged into Janice. Instantly, Janice jerked her arms free of Will's grasp and the two women sprawled on the floor in another flurry of kicking, face-scratching, and hair-pulling.

"Bouncer! Bouncer!" someone shouted.

On the floor, Janice was atop Brenda, slapping her again and again in the face and head. Brenda raised her arms to protect herself against the incoming blows.

Seconds later, the bouncer, a towering hulk of a man, appeared and, grabbing Janice under the arms, pulled her off the other woman.

"That's enough!" he shouted.

Janice stood up, the bouncer holding her waist to restrain her.

Brenda rose to her feet, glared angrily at her adversary, then charged her again. Quickly, the bouncer stepped between the women to fend off the new charge. Then, holding Janice's arm in one hand and Brenda's in the other, he spun both women around and pulled them toward the front door.

"Both of you are out of here," he said. "If you want to fight, you can go out to the parking lot."

Moments later, the three disappeared out the door.

Excitement over and peace restored, the couples resumed dancing, the pool players continued their games, and the Gartman crew returned to their drinks and conversation.

Knox laughed. "Paul, you're something else," he said. "I never seen a man that attracts women the way you do."

"He's a lover boy, all right," Will said.

"Like flies to honey," Pete added. "A real-life Romeo."

Paul shook his head. "Sometimes, it can be a pain," he said.

"You can pass it over to me any time you like," Knox said. "I'd give anything to have a way with women like that."

Another woman, a bar patron waiting to play pool, approached Paul. "You're up," the woman said.

Paul looked over and saw the vacant pool table. "Come on, Knox," he said. "Let's play some pool."

Memories

On Sunday morning, Paul was behind the wheel of a lowboy, a heavy-duty long-bed truck used to transport heavy construction equipment. Hauling eighteen tons of steel was going to make for a slow journey and, since the truck permitted a maximum speed of only sixty miles an hour, it would be two, maybe three hours to Georgia. He settled in for the trip.

During long drives, his mind always wandered back to memories of his childhood. A native of Alabama, Paul had grown up on a small farm north of Birmingham. When he wasn't working in the fields with his father, he was exploring the creeks, valleys, and mountains of his native state. He loved the great outdoors. An only child, his mother had been the most influential person in his early life. An avid reader and one-time teacher, she spent many hours reading to him. By the time Paul was ten, she had read *The Adventures of Huckleberry Finn* and *The Adventures of Tom Sawyer* to him twice. As he grew older, she would pass along the books she had read and, by the time he was a teenager, he had read many of the world classics, including *Treasure Island, Moby Dick, Oliver Twist, Hound of the Baskervilles, The Hunchback of Notre Dame, The Count of Monte Cristo,* and most of the works of Jules Verne.

While he was in junior high, he had fallen in love with poetry and, for his fifteenth birthday, his mother had presented him with a copy of the complete works of Edgar Allan Poe. From the first moment he sat down to read the book, he was enthralled. While he loved the short stories, it was the poems that truly fascinated him. Over and over again, he would read *The Raven*, *The Bells*, and *A Dream within a Dream*, but his all-time favorite was *Annabel Lee*.

Annabel Lee was the story of an unnamed narrator who had found the great love of his life in an idyllic seaside setting. The couple had "loved with a love that was more than love" and swore their undying devotion to one another. Then one night, the sea swept ashore and took his beloved. Over the ensuing years, he slept beside the sea each and every night so he could be near his eternal love. Although he had lost her, she would forever live in his heart.

The final stanza reads:

> *For the moon never beams without bringing me dreams*
> *Of the beautiful Annabel Lee;*
> *And the stars never rise but I feel the bright eyes*
> *Of the beautiful Annabel Lee;*
> *And so, all the night-tide, I lie down by the side*
> *Of my darling- my darling- my life and my bride,*
> *In the sepulchre there by the sea,*
> *In her tomb by the sounding sea.*

Only days after reading the poem, he had memorized it and, over the years, when he was bored or troubled, he would find himself quoting the refrain.

In high school, he had no interest in sports and, while other boys dreamed of becoming doctors, lawyers, and engineers, Paul wanted to pursue his love of books and decided to teach high school English.

"Teaching is an honorable profession," his mother had said. "The pay is not great, but the work is steady and you only work nine months out of the year."

So, after high school, Paul had enrolled at the local college and earned a teaching degree. After a year at a small high school near Pratt City, however, his dream turned to ashes. He hated disciplining students and he dreaded grading papers. He had envisioned himself discussing the fine points of Shakespeare's sonnets to enthusiastic students, but the majority, especially the boys, had little or no interest in literature. Even worse, he hated to be cooped up inside all day. He longed for the great outdoors. At the end of the first year, he wanted out of the teaching profession.

The following summer, while visiting in Birmingham, he bumped into Tom Harmon, an old childhood friend. Tom, a civil engineer, had been working with a highway construction firm near Montgomery and invited Paul to sign on for the summer. *What the hell?* he thought. He knew nothing about highway construction, but the offer would give him something to do and he could make a few extra bucks.

His adventure that summer began as a lark, but proved to be a life-changer. After two weeks as a rod man on a surveying crew, he began driving a water truck. A month later, after befriending the company's veteran heavy equipment operator, he learned to run a motor grader, then shortly afterward, a bulldozer. By the end of the summer, he was a full-fledged heavy equipment operator. Every day was new and different. The pay was good, there was little stress and, best of all, he was working outside. Now, at age thirty-nine, he had been employed at Gartman for fourteen years. Traveling the South and building highways had become his life.

Suddenly, he was jolted back to reality when, upon topping a high point in the highway, he saw a long line of traffic creeping slowly ahead of him. Instantly, he applied the brakes and the rig slowed with a screeching groan. Traffic was moving at a snail's pace. He glanced at a road sign. He was in Valdosta, Ga.

As the line of traffic crept slowly northward, his mind wandered back to the incident at Eddie's. Knox was right. He had always had a special way with women. He wasn't sure why. In high school, girls told him he was handsome and flirted with him, but he didn't dwell on it. He certainly didn't want to exploit it. It seemed too selfish and egotistical. To his mind, the fact that women threw themselves at him was something that just sort of happened.

For no particular reason, the lines from *Annabel Lee* flashed into his head.

For the moon never beams without bringing me dreams of the beautiful Annabel Lee.

And the stars never rise but I feel the right eyes of the beautiful Annabel Lee.

Somehow, the beauty of those words always brought a special peace and comfort. He wasn't sure why, but he was certain of the effect they had.

Paul was well aware that the inspiration for *Annabel Lee* was Virginia Clemm, a distant cousin Poe had taken as a child bride. At the time of the marriage, she was thirteen and he was twenty-seven. Their deep love for one another endured for eleven years, then, at age twenty-four, she died of tuberculosis. Poe, a despondent man by nature, never overcame the loss. After her death, Poe, grew more depressed than ever and sank deeper and deeper into alcohol and died several years later.

Secretly, Paul had always dreamed of meeting his own Annabel Lee, a sensual, younger woman who so overwhelmed his emotions that it was futile to deny the fullness of his love. A woman he could pour himself into without fear of rejection.

A woman who would return his deep, abiding love with the same passion he gave it. A woman he could drown himself in.

On the other hand, he had a deathly fear of the dream. Once, during his teaching days, he had met a tall, slim brunette and, after a few months of dating, he found himself falling head-over-heels in love. Once he saw the depths of the passion he had to give, he quickly ended the relationship. He was deathly afraid of the depths of his love. It was dangerous to give all of yourself to a woman, he told himself. Any woman. He had read too many stories of unrequited love. It was a lot easier to get into a relationship like that than it was to get out, he told himself. Despite this, the dream was still very much alive.

Homestead

As Paul pulled off the main highway and turned west, he wasn't sure how far it was to the company's storage facility. Will had said to take the Duck Springs exit, then go west four miles, and he would see the storage area on the west side of the river. Paul thought Will had said the name of the river was "Alachuma" or "Alachuga" or "Ala" something. He knew it was an Indian name, but he couldn't remember the correct pronunciation or the spelling. He would ask for directions.

Then, as he topped a rise in the road, he saw a woman and a small boy standing at a mailbox. Moments later, the heavy rig slowed with a begrudging groan and finally came to a halt in front of the woman and child.

The woman, who was thumbing through several letters, looked up.

"Hello!" Paul said.

"Good morning!" she replied.

"Can you tell me how to get to the Alachuma River?" he asked.

"You mean the Alachua?" she said.

"Yeah, maybe that's it," Paul said.

She pointed along the highway.

"See that rise in the road?" she said.

Paul squinted into the distance.

"I see it."

"That's the Alachua River," she said. "Runs all the way to Valdosta, then turns south and pours into the Suwanee."

"Like in the song?"

"That's right," she said.

Paul studied the woman for a moment. Late twenties, she was thin, well proportioned, and her long, blonde hair was tied in a ponytail. The child looked thin and sickly.

"You're part of the highway construction company?" she asked finally.

"Yes, ma'am."

"You want to go to the other side of the river," she said. "That's where they've been putting all of the machines. Once you cross the bridge, you'll see it on the right."

That was the information he needed.

"What y'all going to do?" she asked.

"We're going to widen the bridge and make two lanes of the highway into four lanes."

"That'll make it a lot safer," she said.

"We hope so," Paul said.

An awkward silence.

For another long moment, he stared at the woman and child.

"Okay," he said finally. "Thanks for your help."

"You're welcome," she said.

Then, taking the child's hand, she turned and, together, they started walking back along the dirt road to the nearby farmhouse.

For a moment, Paul peered after them, then he gunned the engine and the giant truck and its heavy load slowly groaned up the highway. As she had promised, immediately after crossing the river, he saw an area enclosed by a chain link fence and a sign bearing the company name and logo. Will had given him a key. Five minutes later, the trailer and pan were parked inside the storage area and Paul pulled the bobtail truck back out on the highway. Since there were no motels in Duck Springs, Will had asked Paul to meet him at a truck stop in Albany where he would find rooms for the crew. As he started back to the main highway, he glanced at the homestead where he had seen the woman and child. There was a small farmhouse, a barn and pasture, a garden plot, and a row of ten recently pruned peach trees. Absently, he glanced down the dirt road leading to the farmhouse. It was empty.

* * * *

Cassie Carter and her son, nine-year-old Timmy, had arrived back at the farmhouse. There was never enough time, she thought, as she led her son up the front porch steps and opened the door. She had to clean up the breakfast dishes, wash three loads of clothes, and milk the cow. For three days now, she had been putting off emptying the ashes in the cook stove because she was unable the find the scoop. Twice she had asked Timmy if he had seen it, but he claimed ignorance. As always, the scoop would turn up soon or later. Her husband Austin would be calling around four to check in with her. He was somewhere in Indiana, delivering a load of truck tires. She had to get busy.

After sitting Timmy down in the living room with a coloring book, she went to the kitchen. Twenty minutes later, the breakfast dishes had been washed and put away. As she dried her hands, she remembered the sheets had to be changed. It had been three days.

In the bedroom, she began stripping the bed; first the sheets and then the pillowcases. Finally, carrying a basket heaped high with dirty clothes, she went to the back porch and began stuffing clothes into the washer.

Her proudest possession was the new wringer washer Austin had purchased the previous Christmas. For years, she had boiled the family clothes in an old twenty-gallon wash pot. The new washer was an absolute Godsend. No more building fires, stirring the clothes, and dealing with the black soot that accumulated on the sides of the wash pot. It was 1961 and technology was making life easier for housewives.

Once the clothes were washing, she checked on Timmy. He was still occupied with the coloring book.

"I'm going to milk the cow," she said. "Are you going to wait on the back porch?"

"Yes, Mama," the son replied.

Moments later, she strode across the backyard, milk bucket in hand. At the barn, she took a bucket of feed from the hay room, then emptied it into a trough in the barn hallway. She could see Topsy, the family cow, grazing in the pasture.

"Whoooooo, Topsy!" she called.

Instantly, the cow turned at the sound of her voice and started loping toward the barn.

Five minutes later, Cassie was seated on a stool in the barn hallway, milking. Topsy had dropped a new calf the previous year and Cassie always milked the two large front teats for the family table and saved the two smaller back ones for the calf. After some twenty minutes, the bucket was brimming with fresh, warm milk. She got up, opened the gate to the nearby stall, and let the calf go to the cow.

As she strode back across the yard, lugging the bucket of milk, her son was waiting on the back porch as he often did.

"Mama, can you come and make me a sandwich?" he asked.

"Sure, baby," she replied. "I'll be there. It's time for your medicine."

* * * *

Just after nine p.m., her work finally finished and Timmy asleep, she collapsed on the bed. This was her quiet time, her favorite time of the day when she had no worries or responsibilities toward anyone but herself. It was a time for pampering and self-reflection.

In the distance, she heard the faint rumble of thunder. She got up from the bed and went to the window. Intermittent raindrops were clinking on the windowpanes. The wet clothes she had hung out would have to wait for warm sunshine tomorrow.

Absently, she turned from the window and went to Timmy's room to retrieve the blue spiral-bound notebook she kept hidden among the sheets and pillowcases. Then she returned to the bedroom. The notebook was her journal, her solace at the end of the day. It was here she could pour out her naked thoughts openly and freely without fear of censure or criticism. It was an outlet, a friend she could always talk to and confide in to the fullest. For a moment, she flipped through its pages, then changed her mind. She would make today's entry after a warm bath.

Moments later, in the bathroom, she leaned over the tub and started to run bath water. After removing her panties and bra, she examined her naked body in the mirror. At twenty-six, she was still an attractive woman. There were a few tiny wrinkles at the corners of her eyes, but the skin on her face was still taut and smooth. Her breasts still firm and high, waist trim, hips and legs thin. She wondered why Austin didn't compliment her about her body anymore. When they were dating and after they were married, he would speak admiringly of her breasts and thighs, but after Timmy was born, his compliments had faded away.

Absently, she turned from the mirror and dipped a finger in the bath water to check the temperature. Perfect. She stepped into the bathtub and slowly lowered her body, inch by tantalizing inch, into the soft warmth. Her thoughts wandered back to her childhood.

The youngest of three children, she had grown up in Elberton, a small town in northeast Georgia famous for its granite mines. When she graduated high school, she had few expectations. Her parents had no money for college and, while her brother was destined to spend his life in the granite quarries with his father, the two daughters were expected to find husbands and leave the family home. When Cassie was a senior in high school, her older sister Audrey had married her high school sweetheart and moved to Albany so her husband could work in a mobile home manufacturing plant. Once Cassie graduated high school, Audrey invited her to come to south Georgia, where she found work sewing in a dress shop. The hours were long and the pay was meager. After another worker left the shop to work as a waitress at the local truck stop, Cassie followed. There she met Austin. After they dated for just over a month, he proposed and they were married. She accepted his proposal because she knew he was a good man. Simple and hard working with no vices, he had a good heart and was devoted to his job. Most of all, he represented stability and security.

After her bath, she dried off, put on nightclothes, and crawled into bed. Instinctively, she reached for the notebook and a pen. Pen in hand, she started to write.

April 21, 1961: DeWayne Glover, the son of the owner at Glover's General Store in town, is such a nice man. Today, he gave me almost a dollar off a five-pound sack of flour. These prices these days. A dollar fifty for a five-pound sack of flour and roast pork at 39 cents a pound. Gas costs 31 cents a gallon. I don't know how people make ends meet. DeWayne is also an agent for the insurance company where Austin has his life policy. He comes by every three months to collect. After I bought my groceries, he helped me out to the truck with them. He told me how pretty I was. I liked that. I don't hear that much anymore. He's such a nice man, but I know he's married.

She stopped writing. Outside, the spring rain, which was only a light sprinkle earlier, was steadier now and she could see tiny rivulets of water coursing downward as the heavy droplets pelted the windowpanes.

On rainy nights like this, I feel so alone. I know that my husband must be gone for long periods of time to provide for his family, but I still long for the touch of a man in the night. I'm not sure why Austin has no interest in lovemaking anymore. For some time now, when I approach him to fulfill my womanly needs, he says he is tired and turns away. I'm not sure why. I'm still an attractive woman. At least, I think I am. Lovemaking is almost a chore for him. Despite this, Austin is a good man, a loving father, and devoted husband. I guess I was not meant to have all the things I want in this world. Maybe it was just not meant for me to understand these things.

I'm concerned about Timmy at school. He said one of the older boys pushed him down last week because he wouldn't give up his place in the lunch line. The boy's name was Tommy Elliot. I'm going to have Austin go to the school next week and talk to the principal. It's not fair for older, bigger boys to pick on a smaller child who has the disease that Timmy has.

She stopped writing. Now the rain was pouring down and, whipped by the April winds, it was slapping against the sides of the house. She got out of bed and returned the notebook to Timmy's room where she kept it hidden. Then she returned to bed and flipped off the light.

Runaway Calf

The following morning, promptly at seven, Paul was on a bulldozer, plowing up the vegetation along the north side of the existing highway. All of the vegetation along both sides of the existing highway had to be removed. Any organic matter left in the new base would inevitably rot and create soft spots, which would finally create potholes in the new highway. When he began work, a thick fog had shrouded the roadway, but by late morning, the sun had finally peeped through the smooth, cloudy skies and burned away the mist.

Just after ten a.m., he saw the woman come out of the house with an empty wash basket. Her long, blonde hair waved slightly in the breeze as she took down each article of clothing, folded it, and placed it neatly in the laundry basket. As he watched, he remembered how well proportioned her body was. The shoulders, the breasts, the waist, and legs. Finally, the basket was filled with clean, folded clothes, and she picked it up and started back to the farmhouse.

It was 11:30, almost lunchtime. He had bought a tuna sandwich, chips, pickles, and a soft drink at the motel lunch counter. They were in a cooler on the bulldozer. Finally, just before noon, he shut down the machine, grabbed the cooler, and made a beeline for the big water oak tree that lived just beyond the right-of-way. Once comfortably seated in the shade, he opened the cooler. As he unwrapped the sandwich, he saw the woman come out of the house and go into the barn.

Moments later, she appeared with the calf on a rope. Once she had closed the gate behind her, the calf suddenly broke into a run. For several moments, she ran behind the calf, then, unable to keep pace, she suddenly fell forward, and the calf dragged her across the field. For a moment, Paul thought she would release the rope and let the calf run free, but, for some reason, she was unable to release the rope.

Holy Christ, he thought, she could be killed.

Quickly, he laid aside the sandwich and rushed toward the woman and the calf. Moments later, he slipped through the barbed wire fence and raced across the pasture. Instinctively, he ran in front of the calf and, as it passed, he grabbed the rope and, with all his might, gave it a sudden jerk. Instantly, the calf tumbled to the ground. Seconds later, he was standing over the woman. He could see the rope was twisted around her wrist.

"Are you okay?" he asked.

She didn't answer at first. She was trying to regain her breath.

"Oh, God! I think so," she said. "I didn't realize how strong that calf was."

"Can I help you up?" he asked, offering his hand.

"No, I'm okay," she said. "I just need to catch my breath."

After several more deep breaths, she stood up.

There were lacerations on her face and arms and one deep cut on her right shoulder.

"That's a nasty cut," he said.

She glanced at the cut, then rubbed it with her hand, the fresh blood smearing across her upper arm.

"Here!" he said, producing a handkerchief. "Use this!"

She took the handkerchief and wiped away the blood.

"Hold it on the cut," he said. "It will stop the bleeding."

She did as he instructed.

"I'll put some iodine and a bandage on it when I get back to the house," she said.

"Are you okay now?" he asked.

"I'll be fine," she said. "Would you mind getting the rope off the calf?"

"Sure," he said.

Paul walked across the pasture to the calf, now grazing leisurely in the fresh spring grass along the fence line. The calf flinched momentarily at his approach, but, once he grabbed the rope, he used it to pull the animal to him, then carefully unlooped it from around its neck.

"Thanks for helping me," she said as he handed her the rope.

"You're welcome," he said. "You helped me the other day. Remember?"

"I remember," she said. "What's your name?"

"Paul," he said.

"Paul," she said. "That was my father's name."

There was an uneasy silence.

She looked away.

"Okay, Paul," she said finally. "I've got to get back. Thanks again!"

"You're welcome," he said.

She turned and started back to the farmhouse, the curled rope dangling from her right hand and her left hand holding the handkerchief to the shoulder cut.

"Hey!" he called.

She turned.

"What's your name?"

"Cassie," she said.

"Pleased to meet you, Cassie," he said.

She smiled.

His eyes followed her as she made her way across the pasture, unlocked the gate, and started to the farmhouse. As she mounted the steps on the back porch, he wondered what she would look like naked.

* * * *

Late that night, after Timmy was asleep and she had her bath, Cassie turned to her notebook.

April 24, 1961: Today one of the men who is building the new road saved me from a runaway calf. He might have just saved my life because I was no match for that calf. The man who came to my rescue is called Paul, like my father. He is a handsome man. Tall with pleasant features, he speaks well and carries himself like a man. His brown eyes light up like a little boy's when you ask him a question. I wonder if he's married. He's not wearing a ring. Or ever been married. I could never let Austin know that I was having these kind of thoughts toward another man. I must remember to keep my notebook in a safe place.

Cold Water

The following morning, when Paul brought the bulldozer out of the storage area, he saw a big rig truck parked at the farmhouse. Around ten a.m., a burly man with a beard and wearing a baseball cap and overalls emerged from the house and fired up the old red pickup in the front yard. Paul watched as the pickup, a cloud of red dust boiling behind it, rumbled down the dirt road and pulled out on the highway toward Duck Springs. *That must be her husband*, he thought. *He's a long-haul truck driver.*

Over the remainder of that week, Paul had only seen the woman two times. The first time, around 4:30, he saw her go to the barn, milk bucket in hand, then emerge some twenty minutes later, lugging a bucket of fresh milk. The second time, she came out to work in the garden. Wearing an old-fashioned pioneer bonnet, she worked almost two hours using a hoe to create mounds for tomato plants. He laughed out loud when he saw her in the bonnet. He was reminded of his grandmother. She always wore an old-fashioned bonnet like that when she worked in the garden.

Late that afternoon, the husband started digging postholes in the garden. Paul surmised that the posts would be used for a wire to string pole beans. At quitting time, before he started to the storage area with the bulldozer to clock out, Paul took one final glance at the homestead. The woman was using a hoe to lay out garden rows for planting and the man had erected six posts, three on either end of the garden rows. As Paul started to the company storage area, the husband was tamping the fresh earth around the last post.

* * * *

On Wednesday of the following week, the big rig was gone. Paul was still on the bulldozer, chugging up and down the right-of-ways, plowing up bushes and small trees. Around 7:30, he watched as the woman led the child, books in hand, along the road to the highway. Once the child was on the school bus, she started back to the farmhouse. Slowly, as if she feared what she would see, she turned and looked toward Paul. For a long moment, she peered at him, then when she saw he was looking back, she quickly looked away. *That's a good sign*, he thought. It was the first time she had looked toward him in over a week.

At lunch, he was sitting under the water oak, eating. At the homestead, he heard the slam of a closing door. He looked up and saw her coming across the pasture. She was wearing a blue print dress, her hair was in a ponytail, and she was carrying something. He watched as she made her way across the pasture and slipped through the barbed wire fence.

"Good morning," she said.

"Good morning," he replied.

"I wanted to return your handkerchief and bring you some cold water. I know it gets hot out here."

"Yes, it does," he said. "And my cooler isn't that good."

She handed him the clean handkerchief.

He examined it.

"Just like new," he said, stuffing the handkerchief in his shirt pocket.

She handed him a quart fruit jar filled with ice and cold water.

"Thanks," he said, placing the water on the ground beside him. "I think it's going to reach ninety today."

He looked up at her.

"You want to sit for a spell?" he said.

"No, I'll just stand."

He searched his mind for a subject.

"I see you laying off the rows for a garden," he said. "You're going to have pole beans and tomatoes. What else you going to have?"

"Going to have okra, squash, sweet corn, and some eggplant. Eggplants don't do well in south Georgia, but I'm going to try 'em. The ones I had last year grew to about half size, then started to rot. Do you know about gardening?"

"Oh yes," he said. "When I was a boy in Alabama, I spent many happy hours in the garden with my mother."

She looked at him. "You from Alabama?"

He nodded.

"My mama used to say everybody from Alabama was crazy."

He laughed. "Why would she say something like that?" he asked. "You ever been to Alabama?"

"Not exactly," she said.

"What do you mean, 'not exactly'?"

She lingered for a moment. "When I was growing up in north Georgia, my family used to go down to Columbus to visit my Aunt Bessie. She was my mother's sister and they lived on the banks of the Chattahoochee River. That's the line between Alabama and Georgia."

"I know it well," Paul said. "There's an army base there."

"Me and my cousins would play along the banks of the river, fishing and swimming and picnicking. From time to time, we would look across the river to the Alabama side."

She stopped.

"And...?"

"Well, on the Georgia side, everybody I knew was God-fearing folks. They went to church and stayed at home and worked and took care of their families."

"And on the Alabama side?"

"There was a honky-tonky on the side of the mountain and all those people ever did was laugh and dance and drink all night and all day. Even after everybody else was asleep in the wee hours, cars would be going in and out and you could hear loud music and people laughing."

A pause.

"That's why your mama said everybody from Alabama was crazy?"

She nodded.

He laughed. "Your aunt just happened to live across the river from one of those all-night honky-tonks in Phenix City," he said. "There are lots of good people in Alabama."

She peered at him.

"Well, I'm not crazy," he said. "At least, I hope not."

"No," she said. "You seem like a nice person."

His mind searched for a new subject. "That was your husband digging the postholes for the pole beans?"

She nodded.

He could see he had touched a nerve.

"I'm glad you brought this cold water," he said, changing the subject. "The ice in my cooler don't last long in this sun." He reached for the cooler. "Look at this thing," he said, opening the lid.

She stepped forward to examine the cooler.

"I think the seal is broken," he said. "It just won't keep things cold."

She knelt and curiously ran her finger around the edges. "Yeah, I see what you mean," she said.

He took her hand and guided it along the edges of the cooler lid.

"See how loose the seal is," he said. "It's never going to keep things cold with a seal like that."

As he held her wrist, she looked fearfully into his eyes. He could feel her hand trembling. Suddenly, she pulled her hand out of his grasp and stood up.

"Well, I've got to go now," she said.

"Thanks for the water," he said.

"You're welcome."

She studied him for a moment.

"Are you married?" she asked.

"No, I'm a single man," he replied. "I was engaged once when I was in my twenties, but it didn't work out."

"Do you like peach cobbler?"

"I love peach cobbler," he said.

"I'm baking one," she said. "Want me to bring you a piece?"

"Oh, I'd love that," he said.

An awkward silence.

"Well, I've got to get back," she said.

"Thanks," he said. "I can't wait to taste your peach pie."

She smiled.

"Tomorrow," she said.

Quickly, she turned and headed back up the embankment toward the pasture. He watched as she slipped through the barbed wire fence and started across the pasture. Before she opened the gate, she turned and looked at him. She waved. He waved back.

May 4, 1961: Today, I talked with Paul again. What a beautiful man! Quiet, smart, and he knows a lot about the world. Lots more than me. His brown eyes are like pools of muddy water that I could fall into without even trying. His smile is so easy and caring that I fear what might happen if I am near him for too long. His name is Paul like my father, but he is a totally different man than my father. Although he is strong and looks like a man's man, I can see that he has lots of feelings inside. Feelings he is not ashamed to show other people. His arms and neck are strong and muscular and he seems very intelligent.

When he touched my hand today, I could feel shivers run up and down my spine. I've got to control this lust inside me, although I'm not sure I can. The need is so great. I promised him a piece of my peach pie. I'll take it to him tomorrow. I'll see how much control I have.

Peach Pie

Promptly at seven the next morning, Paul was back on the bulldozer, plowing up vegetation along the north side of the existing highway. When he fired up the bulldozer, he knew the day was going to be hot. Skies were clear and the bright sun of early morning promised more heat as it rose higher and higher in the eastern sky. As he made pass after pass, he glanced up intermittently toward the homestead. Around 7:30, she walked her son to the highway to catch the school bus. Once the child was safely on the bus, he watched as she walked back to the farmhouse. She didn't look toward him. By midmorning, he had cleared more than a hundred-yard swath along the highway's edge. Finally, just before noon, he shut down the bulldozer, retrieved his cooler, and took a seat under the big water oak near the river. Ten minutes later, he looked up and saw the woman coming across the pasture. She was carrying a covered plate. He smiled to himself. *This one is going to be too easy*, he thought. *Even better, there is going to be some home-cooked food included.*

"Good morning," she said.

"Hello," he replied. "I see you kept your promise."

"Yes," she said, handing him the dish. "There's a fork in there. I didn't think you would have one."

"Your timing is perfect," he said. "I just finished my lunch."

She watched as he removed the covering from the peach pie.

"Looks good," he said. "Crust is just brown enough."

"I hope you like it."

Using the fork, he cut off a piece of the pie and tasted it.

She waited.

"It's delicious," he said. "Where do you get peaches this time of year?"

"Oh, they're canned," she said. "Fresh peaches won't be here until July. Every year, I get three or four bushels off those trees. That's more than enough for forty to fifty quarts of canned peaches."

He laughed. "I bet you learned to can from your mother," he said.

She smiled. "Yep," she said with a smile. "My mama taught me most everything I know. How to can, how to cook, how to milk, how to garden, how to sew. I learned a lot from my mother."

"My mother taught me a lot too," he said. "She taught me my love of books. Even now, I still miss her."

"You didn't learn anything from your daddy?"

He paused. "I learned things from my father," he said. "Things like farming and working the fields, but my father didn't have any interest in book learning. He read things like *Country Gentleman* to try to be a better farmer, but my mother, she wanted to know about things beyond our farm."

As she listened, she felt oddly comfortable with him. The tone of his voice was soothing and receptive.

"What about you?" he asked. "What did you learn from your father?"

He cut off another bite of the peach pie.

"My father?" she said. "I didn't have a father."

"Your parents were divorced?"

"Oh, no! Not that!" she said. "My father was always there in the house, but he didn't have time for me. All of his time was spent at work and taking care of business. Sometimes, he would go days and days without even speaking to me. Only person he had time for was my older brother."

"That's too bad," he said. "A young girl needs to be close to her father."

She didn't answer right away.

"Did you miss not being close to your father?"

"Many, many times," she said.

He could hear the bitterness in her voice. He waited for her to continue.

Her eyes turned from him and peered off into the distance.

"I always wondered what it would be like to have a father that would spend time with me," she continued. "A father that would come to me and say 'Let's talk' or 'Let's go fishing' or 'I love you.' When I was in school, I heard other girls tell about how their fathers had given them gifts and taken them to the movies and shared secrets with them. In high school, my friend Wanda Blevins' father would take her to the local drug store for an ice cream soda every Sunday afternoon. He even played basketball with her in the backyard. I couldn't imagine my father doing something like that."

A long silence.

He could see she was lost in thought.

"What kind of work did he do?"

"He worked in the granite mines," she said. "He spent all day cutting blocks of granite out of the mountain."

He looked at her.

"As a father," she continued, "he was as cold and hard as the granite he cut out of the ground."

Again, he could hear the bitterness in her voice. "That's too bad," he said.

Suddenly, she realized she had spilled her most private thoughts to him. "Sorry, I got carried away," she said.

"That's okay," he said. "I'm glad you told me about you and your father."

"You're really easy to talk to," she said.

Awkward silence.

"How's the pie?"

"Oh, it's great," he said, taking the last bite.

"Well, I've got to go now," she said.

He stood up.

Suddenly, she was aware of how tall he was. He was well over six feet and towered over her. His strong neck and lean face were dark from the constant exposure to the sun.

"I see the cut on your shoulder is healing," he said.

He stepped forward.

"Can Dr. Paul examine your wound?"

She laughed at his easy manner. "Sure," she replied. "Go ahead, Dr. Paul."

His finger ran around the edge of the bandage. As he touched her bare arm, she felt her body suddenly come alive with sensation. She was afraid to look into his eyes.

"You need a fresh bandage," he said. "I've got a first-aid kit on the dozer."

"No," she said. "You don't have to do that."

"It will only take a minute," he said.

Moments later, he returned with the first aid kit. Quickly he removed the old bandage, then applied antibiotic ointment and a new bandage.

"There you go," he said. "Now you're good as new."

"Thanks, Dr. Paul," she said. "Is there anything else I should do?"

"Yeah," he replied. "Take two aspirin and call me tomorrow."

She laughed at his playfulness.

Suddenly, looking straight into her eyes, he stepped forward. As they stood facing one another, he gently grasped each of her wrists with his hands and pulled her toward him. She suddenly felt an electric excitement course through her body.

"You're such a beautiful woman," he said.

His lips moved to kiss her. She turned away, but his lips followed hers and before she could resist further, their lips met. For a moment, she didn't respond, but her body told her it was useless to resist. Suddenly, she could feel herself letting go. She could feel the store of passion inside her body yearning to erupt. Seconds later, she was returning his kisses with the same desire he was giving them. She was breathing hard.

He reached for her bosom.

"No! No!" she said, pulling away. "Not here! Not now!"

"What's wrong?" he asked.

"Tonight," she said. "Tonight at the river."

"Where?"

"See the cane break?" she said, pointing in the distance.

Paul turned and peered toward the river. He could see the tops of a bamboo grove.

"I see it," he said. "What time?"

"It'll be after my son is in bed," she said. "Around 8:30."

"I'll be waiting," he said.

She turned quickly and started back up the embankment.

"Don't forget your dish," he said.

She giggled like a little girl, then she strode back to him and took the dish. As she turned, he grabbed her wrist and spun her around to face him. For a moment, their trembling lips met again, then she pulled away.

"Tonight!" she said.

Secret Meeting

That afternoon after work, Paul returned to his motel room, shaved, and showered. As he stood in front of the mirror shaving, he wondered what he was about to embark upon. Once he was dressed, he ate a fried fish sandwich at the motel restaurant. Back in his room, he tried to watch *I Love Lucy* on the television, but flipped it off after only a few minutes. His mind was distracted by the meeting. Just after eight p.m., he went to the truck and started the drive to the construction site. As he drove, he wondered what she looked like unclothed. He couldn't wait to see those wonderful shoulders, those breasts, and that waist in their naked loveliness.

It was eight miles from the motel to the company storage facility. Upon arrival, he parked the truck and locked it. Then he crossed the highway and scrambled down the embankment to the path alongside the river. He had brought a flashlight, but a full moon provided enough light for him to make his way along the trail. As he walked, his nose suddenly caught the distinctively sweet scent of wild pears. He stopped and looked around him. To the left, hidden among the foliage, he saw two wild pear trees. Huge blooms were sprouting on the branches and they would be bearing fruit in a few weeks. Quickly, he turned and continued along the water's edge. Finally, he could see the cane break ahead.

The stand of bamboo was more than twenty feet high and stretched along the river's edge for twenty, maybe thirty yards.

At some point in the past, enough bamboo had been cleared from the water's edge to launch a boat into the river. Paul could see where the bamboo had been thinned to allow access to the river and gravel had been dumped along the water's edge to provide a firm footing for a vehicle and a boat trailer. In the bright moonlight, he could see a path leading through the broomsage patch to the barn. He looked at his watch. It was 8:20.

Five minutes later, he heard the sound of footsteps and the rustle of broomsage along the path. When he looked up, he saw her silhouette coming toward him. As she drew closer, he could see she was carrying something.

"Hi," he said. "What did you bring?"

"Chicken and dumplings and fresh cornbread."

"What else?"

"A quilt."

He took the quilt and the food.

"Wait just a moment," he said.

Along the river's edge, a tree had fallen into the water. With the river's constant rise and fall, thousands of dried leaves had accumulated within its naked branches. Quickly, he gathered several handfuls of leaves and placed them alongside the log, then he spread the quilt across the leaves.

"Now we'll have a soft place to lay our heads," he said.

"You think of everything."

"So do you," he said.

No further words needed to be spoken. Quickly, he took her into his arms and began kissing her. The need she had felt earlier with his first kiss came roaring back with full intensity and she sensed herself melting away with his kisses. Moments later, both were naked. *Oh, great God*, he thought when he saw her body in the soft moonlight. As she lay back on the quilt and beckoned him to come to her, he remembered the statue of Venus on a half shell with its delicate form and features. The soft shoulders, the childlike innocence, the quiet beauty. Moments later, they were thrusting their bodies together as if their very lives depended on making two bodies into one. It was as if they were trying to become one person and never again be lonely or without love.

Thirty minutes later, their passion spent, they lay naked on the quilt. High overhead, the moon was a shining ball of yellow light.

"Look at that moon," she said.

He peered skyward through the treetops.

"Absolutely beautiful," he said. "You know, President Kennedy says they're going to send men to walk on it in ten years."

She looked at him.

"Oh, flitter," she said. "I heard that on television, but I don't believe it. How're they going to get up there?"

"They're going to build rockets and fly up there."

"That's crazy," she said. "I'll believe it when I see it."

"Science is doing some pretty incredible things these days."

"I know," she said. "But going to moon? That's all God's work up there. Human beings have no business messing with all that."

"Are you a religious person?" he asked.

"Not really," she said. "I just believe that some things in this world are sacred and should be left alone."

"I see your point," he said, his eyes moving to the covered dishes.

"Let's eat," he said. "I'm hungry."

She rose to a sitting position on the quilt and began unwrapping the two bowls of chicken and dumplings and cornbread. The bowls were still warm. She handed one bowl and a tablespoon to him, then watched as he uncovered the dish and began to eat. She felt so comfortable with him. Now that he had touched the secret places of her body to his, she somehow felt she had known him all of her life. She loved the freedom she felt when she was near him.

"How's the chicken and dumplings?" she asked.

"Great!" he said. "Just the right amount of black pepper. Black pepper is what makes good chicken and dumplings."

Moments later, he finished the dish.

She watched as he put the bowl to his lips and drank the last bit of broth, then got up.

"Where are you going?"

"I'm going to the river to wash the bowl and get a drink of water."

"There's a natural spring in the broomsage patch," she said.

"Really?" he asked. "Come on; let's get some fresh water."

"Like this?" she asked, referring to their nakedness.

He laughed at her concern.

"Of course, like this," he said. "We'll play like Adam and Eve."

She laughed at his playfulness.

He retrieved the flashlight.

"Here," he said, handing her the flashlight. "You know the way."

Moments later, she was running naked up the trail through the broomsage. He was close behind. Finally, she stopped.

"There," she said, shining the light on a gurgling, natural spring embedded in the hillside. The many years of the gushing water had eroded the soil and created a small gully in front of the spring.

"My God! How beautiful!" he said. "Hold the light. I want to get a drink."

Seconds later, in his nakedness, he knelt in front of the spring, catching water in his cupped hands and drinking it.

"It's so sweet and pure," he said.

Finally, after he had enough, he playfully threw a spate of water toward her. The fresh water splashed on her face and breasts.

"That's cold!" she said, drawing back.

He stood up.

She laughed.

"Look at your knees," she said.

He looked down. Both knees were a solid brown color from having been sunk in the mud in front of the spring. He laughed, then standing close to the spring, he splashed handful after handful of water on his knees until they were clean. He stood to face her. Their eyes met, their lips met, and she felt another rush of raw desire surge through her body.

"Come on," she said. "Let's go back to the quilt."

Together, naked and hand-in-hand, they raced back along the path through the broomsage and fell together on the old quilt. Moments later, they were thrusting their bodies together again. Her body was afire and, as wave after wave of sensations reached a floodtide, her back arched suddenly and she let out a muffled scream as her body released its store of passion.

Finally, breathing hard, hearts racing and passion spent, they stopped and lay back on the quilt to rest. Suddenly, in the quietness, he heard movement in the nearby brush.

"Shhh!" he said, raising himself to a sitting position.

"What is it?"

"Give me the flashlight," he whispered.

Quickly, he took the flashlight and shined it in the direction of the sound. Along the water's edge, he could see a stand of ten to twelve dogwood trees. As he steadied the flashlight beam among the young dogwoods, he suddenly saw three sets of eyes reflecting back at him.

Instantly, he drew back. "What is that?" he asked.

She laughed. "Those are white-tail deer," she said. "It's a mother and two fawns."

He shined the light closer. Now he could make out the deer peering at them.

"That's absolutely incredible," he said. "I've never seen deer so tame."

He stood up and peered into the darkness toward the other side of the river.

"Can anybody see us here?"

"Who's going to see us?" she said. "We have no neighbors for almost half a mile. All of that over there," she said, indicating the other side of the river, "is all government land. The only person within half a mile is Timmy and he's sound asleep."

She stood and peered across the moonlit river.

"The river is really wide here," she said. "Every winter, the ducks stop here during their migration. In December and January, there are thousands and thousands of ducks. Just a-quacking and squawking and flapping their wings like there was no tomorrow."

He looked at her. "That's why they call it Duck Springs?"

She nodded. "It's really something to see," she said. "When me and my husband first moved here, hunters would sneak on to the other side to shoot the ducks, then the federal authorities came and it all stopped. Do you like to hunt?"

He looked at her. "I couldn't kill another living thing," he said. "It's bad karma."

"Bad what?"

"Bad karma," he said.

"I've heard that word, but I don't know what it means."

"Karma is a law of nature," he said. "Karma means that when you do bad things, bad things happen to you. When you do good things, good things happen to you."

"The Bible says the same thing," she said.

"How do you mean?"

"In Galatians, it says, 'What you sow is what you will reap.'"

"Yeah," he said thoughtfully. "I guess it is the same idea." He peered at her. "For a country woman that's never traveled much, you're smart."

"I never thought of myself as all that smart," she said. "I was a fair student in high school, but I'm always trying to learn new things. I like to read books and try new things."

"What books have you read?"

"My all-time favorite is *Gone with the Wind*," she said. "I've read it cover to cover at least three times. I tried to read the *Wizard of Oz* to my son, but he couldn't follow it. Also, I love short stories."

"Ever read Poe?" he asked.

"I read *The Raven* when I was in high school. His stories are too scary for me. I'm afraid I'll have nightmares if I read that stuff."

He laughed. "Yeah," he said, "Poe can be really scary at times. Ever read *Annabel Lee*?"

"No," she replied.

"I'll have to read it to you sometime."

A long pause.

"Shhhhhh!!" she said. "Listen!"

"What is it?" he asked.

"Listen," she said. "Hear that whippoorwill?"

He listened. Somewhere nearby, he could hear the bird's intermittent call. He smiled. "Know what he's saying?"

"No," she replied.

"Chip fell out of the white oak. Chip fell out of the white oak."

"What?"

"Chip fell out of the white oak," he replied. "Say it real fast. Again and again."

"Chipfelloutofthewhiteoak!" she said aloud several times. "Chipfelloutofthewhiteoak!"

She smiled at the recognition. The words, when said rapidly, perfectly mimicked the whippoorwill's call

"Yeah," she said. "You're right. Where did you hear that?"

"From my father," he said. "When I was a small boy."

She said it again and again. She had learned something new. "I'll always remember that," she said. "I'm always learning new things from you."

She arose from the quilt.

"Where are you going?" he asked.

"To wash off in the river."

"Can I help?"

She laughed. "Of course," she said, offering her hand.

Together, hand-in-hand, they waded into the clear river water, their naked bodies silhouetted in the moonlight. The water was cool and refreshing to their bodies. Finally, they stopped and he turned to face her. Then, for a long moment, his hands on her waist, he peered into her eyes.

"What are you thinking?" she asked.

"I'm thinking that I could fall madly in love with you."

She laughed. "Don't you think it's a little early?" she asked. "This is only the first time we've been together."

"It never hurts to dream," he said.

Awkward silence.

"I wanted to ask you about your son," he said.

She turned away. "I don't want to talk about my son," she said. Suddenly, she turned from him. "I need to go," she said. "My husband will be back tomorrow."

He knew he had hit a nerve.

"I'm sorry," he said. "I didn't mean to offend you."

"It's okay," she said, turning from him and heading to shore. "You didn't offend me. I do need to be going."

Moments later, they were back on shore, drying off their bodies with the old quilt.

"When can I see you again?" he asked.

"I'm not sure," she said. "I'll leave you a message."

"Where?"

"In the peach tree," she said. "The one on the end closest to the barn. I'll leave you a message in a fruit jar."

"How will I know when you've left a message?"

"Look for the calf," she said. "If the calf is in the front pasture, you'll know there is a message."

He nodded.

Both were fully dressed again.

"Don't ever go near the house in daytime," she said. "Especially on weekends. Timmy might see you."

"I won't," he promised.

Moments later, she had folded the quilt and gathered the empty dishes. She stood before him, ready to leave.

"One thing!" he said.

"What's that?"

"I enjoyed you," he said.

She smiled.

"I enjoyed you too," she replied.

"Can I get one final kiss?"

"Sure," she said.

She held her face up to him. He kissed her lightly on the lips, then watched as she turned and started back up the path through the broomsage. Suddenly, she turned.

"One more thing," she said.

"What's that?"

"Next time, you'll have to use protection."

"Okay," he said.

Quickly, she turned and started up the trail again. For a moment, he could see her silhouette against the night sky, then she faded into the darkness. As he started back up the river trail, he wondered what secret she was hiding about her son.

That night, Cassie made a new entry in her journal.

May 7, 1961: Oh great God, what am I getting into here? I was with another man tonight and, even now, I still feel his kisses. I feel his hands on my body, feeding the passion deeper and deeper within me. All of my body is aching to be with this man again. This man has touched parts of me I didn't even know I had. What's happening to me? I think I'm going crazy with lust for this man. I'm afraid of what's happening to me. I can't wait to be with him again.

Dogwood Princess

For Paul, the first meeting had been like a dream, an incredible fantasy conjured by some magical sorcerer. Being with a woman so beautiful and loving her with such desire and energy was like a lyric poem he had read in a forgotten book many, many years ago. It was not the wham-bam-thank-you-ma'am experience he had had with so many of the women he had picked up in bars and restaurants over the years. His time with Cassie had been lovemaking to be treasured. It was a sacred experience, something truly precious to be cherished and remembered.

Three weeks passed. Every morning when he arrived at work, the big rig truck would be gone. Then, every afternoon at quitting time, it would be back in the front yard. *Her husband must be making short daily runs,* he thought. Every day, he watched as she went about her daily routine. Some days, he would see her in her pioneer bonnet, working in the garden. The pole beans were coming up and he watched as she got down on her hands and knees to curl the young sprouts around the placed strings. Some days, he would watch as she hoed away the weeds from the sweet corn and young tomato plants. Other days, he would see her at the clothesline, hanging out wet clothes or taking down and folding dried ones. Some days, he would see her in the late afternoon going to milk the cow. Each and every time he saw her, his body ached for hers.

Meanwhile, the Duck Springs project was progressing well. It was the last week in May and both sides of the existing highway had been cleared of vegetation and leveled to grade specifications. Now the massive task of building the base for the new lanes and shoulders was beginning. Thousands of tons of raw earth would have to be moved from the nearby public lands and dumped alongside the two existing lanes. Day after day, Paul made pass after pass in an earthmover, scooping up giant bites of earth, then delivering it to a central pile for the dump trucks. During the second week in May, the cranes had arrived to drive the pilings for the new bridge structures. After only a week, the pilings were in and the giant steel beams, which would serve as supports for the new bridge lanes, were welded into place. Now, carpenters were building the forms that would hold the concrete to strengthen and fortify the bridge supports.

When he was working on the west side of the river, Paul only had intermittent views of the homestead. The existing bridge structure and the tall water oaks along the river's edge blocked his view, but each and every time he had a window, his eyes peered anxiously at the homestead to see if the big rig was gone. His heart yearned to see the calf in the front pasture or the sight of her going to the peach tree.

It was the second week in June and the entire countryside was alive with spring greenery. Along the river, the leaves and foliage were now colored in a patchwork of deep green. Dogwoods, poplars, sweet gums, and water oaks were brilliantly alive with color. The peach trees were in bloom and the sweet scent of the pink blossoms carried across the river. The days were warm and the buzz of insects filled the air. It was a glorious time.

On Wednesday of that week, the big rig was gone. That morning, he had watched her deliver her son to the school bus, then emerge some two hours to work in the garden. Just before quitting time, he saw her going to the barn to milk the cow. Seconds later, she emerged from the barn hallway and went to the peach tree. His heart raced with excitement. Some twenty minutes later, the calf was in the front pasture.

That night, just before darkness fell, he drove to the company storage area. Making his way along the river's edge, he finally arrived at the cane break. Then he started to the peach tree. As he approached, he could see the tree had three major branches and nestled in the crux was a fruit jar. Eagerly, he opened it.

Friday night. 8:30. Will bring food.

His heart was racing as he replaced the fruit jar. Quickly, he made his way back along the river's edge to his truck. Once inside, he looked at the note again. As he read it again for confirmation, he could feel his passion rising at the thought of being with her again. The memories of running naked through the broomsage and wading into the warm river water came rushing back into his memory. He was going to be with her again.

Thursday passed and all day Friday, as he maneuvered the earthmover along the west side of the river, he watched for any activity at the homestead. She never appeared. He wondered if there was a problem. After work that afternoon, he returned to the motel room, showered and shaved, and drove to the storage facility. As he made his way along the river's edge, several white tail deer scampered off the trail. It was a beautiful night. High overhead, the moon was a golden disk of luminescence. He had brought the flashlight, but there was plenty of light. Moments later, he arrived at the point where he had seen the wild pear trees. He stopped. Both trees were loaded with soft, ripe pears. He knew he had to share with her. Quickly, he stepped off the path and gathered ten to twelve pears, carefully selecting the softest, ripest ones. Finally, both hands and arms full of wild pears, he continued along the river's edge.

At the cane break, he stopped and looked at his watch. It was 8:20. He peered up the trail through the broomsage. All was quiet. Restless, he took a seat on the log that was leaning into the water. As he waited, his nose caught the scent of dogwood blossoms. Just beyond the log, the dogwood trees where they had seen the deer were heavy with white fragrant blossoms. At 8:45, he thought there must be a problem, then, seconds later, he heard the sound of footsteps along the path and the rustle of broomsage. When she appeared, his heart soared with delight.

"Sorry I'm late," she said breathlessly. "Timmy was being difficult and didn't want to go to sleep."

"That's okay," he said. "I'm just happy to see you."

She had brought the old quilt and two covered dishes.

"What's for dinner?" he asked, taking the quilt.

"Fried chicken, green beans, and mashed potatoes," she replied.

"With gravy?"

"No gravy," she said. "I was afraid it would run into the green beans."

He took the dishes and set them aside. Then he gathered more leaves from the fallen tree and spread the quilt over it.

Then he turned to her.

At the very sight of him, she felt a rush of raw desire shoot through her body. She rushed into his arms.

"Oh, God! I need you!" she said. "I need you so."

Quickly, they undressed one another and fell naked together on the old quilt. As they thrust their bodies together again and again with a time-honored rhythm, all of the stored passion of the past few weeks was released. Finally, hearts racing and breathing hard, they stopped. For a long moment, they were quiet. Both were lying on their backs, peering up at the night sky.

"Do you know the stars?" he asked.

She peered into the night sky at the twinkling stars.

"Let's see," she said. "There's the North Star, the Big Dipper, and Cassiopeia. Over to the right, I see Orion."

"Do you know the stars in Orion?"

"Well, the star at the very top is his head. The two stars below are his shoulders, the three stars in the middle are his belt, and the two bottom stars are his feet."

"Do you know what the stars between his legs represent?"

She giggled with delight and looked at him.

"That's the tip of his sword," he said quickly with a laugh. He looked at her.

"You were going to say something else, weren't you?"

"How would you know what I was going to say?"

"I just know," he said.

They were quiet for a moment.

Finally, he broke the silence. "My mama used to say that if you looked at the North Star for a full minute, then made a wish, that wish would come true."

"Oh really?" she said. "Want to give it a try?"

"Sure," he said. "You go first."

She peered into the night sky at the pole star for a long moment.

"There!" she said.

"What did you wish?"

"I wished that I could go to Atlanta," she said.

"That's all?" he asked. "You just want to go to Atlanta?"

"I've never been to Atlanta," she said.

He laughed.

"You have to understand," she said. "I'm just a simple country girl stuck out here in the middle of nowhere. I haven't traveled the world like you."

He didn't reply. Finally, she spoke up. "Now it's your turn," she said. "You make a wish."

He peered into the night sky for a long moment, then turned to her.

"What did you wish for?" she asked.

"That I could be forever on this earth right beside you like I am right now."

"You're a dreamer," she said.

"You wouldn't like that?"

"Oh, yeah," she said. "It's a nice thought, but in the real world, I'm married to another man."

It was a sobering thought.

"Yeah, I know," he said. "I can dream, can't I?"

She could see that she had burst his bubble. She studied him for a long moment. "At least you have a romantic side to you," she said. "I'll say that for you. I have never known a man that could make fun out of loving like you. I love that side of you so much."

He smiled.

"Want to have some more fun?" he asked.

"What do you mean?"

"Lie back on the quilt for me," he said. "I want to make a princess out of you."

"How are you going to do that?"

"Just lie back on the quilt and let me do what I want to do," he said.

She lay submissively on the quilt, then watched as he stepped to the nearby dogwood tress and began gathering the fragrant blossoms. One by one, he plucked the flowers and placed them in the crux of his arm. Finally, after gathering some forty to fifty flowers, he returned to the quilt and dumped them beside her.

"Now lie still for me," he said.

She lay perfectly still, her naked body shining in the bright moonlight. Carefully, he began decorating her body with the dogwood flowers. He started with her face, lacing the stems of the blossoms into her hair. One by one, he placed the flowers symmetrically until her face was framed with a semicircle of the flowers. As he decorated her body, she felt a deep passion slowly welling within her. Once her face was finished, he moved to her breasts and delicately placed the blossoms around the soft mounds of flesh to form a ring of flowers around each one. Once her breasts were finished, he placed a single large bloom directly on her navel. Then, like a sculptor who had created his masterpiece, he stood up and peered down at her.

"You're so beautiful," he said. "So incredibly beautiful."

Then, he knelt on the quilt and slowly started to run his fingertips lightly across her inner thighs, lingering slowly across her skin. Then his fingers moved upward with his lips leading the way. She felt an electric tingle in her nipples and a growing warmth between her legs. His leading lips nudged aside the blossom on her navel. He licked the soft flesh around her navel then continued up her body to her breasts. Her nipples were hard and erect like little stones. Gently he licked the soft undersides of her breasts, nudging away the blossoms as if he was preferring her body to the fragrant flowers. As his lips brushed across her nipples, she was absolutely wild with desire. His gentle touch and the smell of the dogwoods had driven her need beyond its limits.

"Oh God, Paul," she said. "I've got to have you. I can't wait."

The fire inside her was about to explode.

Then, ever so tenderly, he softly began licking her nipples.

"Oh, Paul, please," she begged. "Please let me have it. I want you. I need you."

Now he was nibbling softly at her neck and she was unable to contain herself any longer. Suddenly, she raised her upper body and threw off the remaining dogwood blossoms. Her eyes were aflame with desire as she grasped his waist and pulled his body into hers.

"Now!" she said. "Now!"

As he thrust his body into hers at that moment, he knew this was lovemaking for all eternity. Being with this woman was the end-all and be-all of lovemaking. This was the kind of lovemaking he had always dreamed of. As their bodies moved together with a time-honored rhythm, the rising floodtide of sensations caused her back to arch and she screamed. It was a primal animal scream that echoed through the trees and across the river, calling out to all living things. Finally, smelling of raw sex and dogwood blossoms, they stopped to rest. It was several minutes before either spoke.

"Never have I had a release like that," she said finally. "I didn't know I was even capable of a release like that."

He was lying on his back on the quilt, trying to regain his breath.

"Oh, God, I love being with you," he said.

"Me too," she replied.

Ten minutes later, their passion spent, they lay naked on the quilt. High overhead, the moon was a glowing yellow ball in the night sky. The air was filled with the croaking of frogs from along the river. They started to eat. The chicken and mashed potatoes were cold, but tasted good with the fresh water they had retrieved from the spring. As he ate, he remembered how everything always seemed to taste better outdoors. Suddenly, he heard a sound along the path beside the river.

"Look," he said, nodding with his head toward the path. "We've got company."

She turned. The same deer and two fawns they had seen a month earlier were standing at the edge of the cane break, peering at them. Finally, after finishing the last bit of cornbread, he turned to her.

"I brought dessert," he said.

"What?" she asked.

"I picked fresh wild pears from a tree I found down the trail," he said.

He got up from the quilt and retrieved one of the pears. She examined the ripe, perfectly formed fruit, then she looked playfully at him.

"Adam, my darling," she asked. "Would you like a taste of my apple?"

He smiled, then knelt beside her on the quilt.

"Of course, Eve, my darling," he replied, taking a seat beside her. "Nothing would please me more than to taste your apple."

She held the wild pear and he took a bite.

"Now I will be yours for all time," he said, chewing the sweet fruit. "I will forever own your body and you shall forever own mine and we shall live forever in our beautiful Garden of Eden."

He stood up and made a melodramatic gesture with his hand.

"Look upon our beautiful garden," he said, with obvious melodrama. "It was created by the hand of God and exists only for us and our pleasure."

He pointed to the deer.

"These are the wild beasts in our garden," he said. "They are the beautiful gifts God has given."

He pointed to the pears.

"Our garden is filled with succulent fruit for our lips."

He gestured toward the water.

"And this river is the great sea that guards our lovely garden," he said. "And we shall live forever in our great paradise of fruit and natural beauty...."

Suddenly, realizing he had gone from the sublime to the ridiculous, she burst out in uproarious laughter. Then, realizing the same, he burst into uproarious laughter and they fell together in one another's arms on the quilt.

"Sometimes, you're too much," she said.

He laughed. "Yeah," he said. "Sometimes, I do go overboard." He turned and looked into her eyes. "God, I love being with you," he said. "I feel so free and unlimited when I'm with you."

"I feel that too," she said. She got up from the quilt.

"Where are you going?"

"Let's go wash off in the river," she said. "Then I've got to go."

Ten minutes later, they were dressed again and preparing to say good-bye.

"One last kiss," he said.

She raised her lips to his, then he held her tightly in his arms. Finally, she released the embrace.

"Oh great God," she said, looking into his eyes. "What are we doing? Tell me what we are doing."

"I don't know," he said. "But I don't want it to ever stop."

"Where is this going? How will it end?" she asked.

He didn't reply.

She shook her head in indecision, then looked away.

"When can I see you again?"

"I'll leave you a message," she said.

"I hope it's soon," he replied.

"I'll do the best I can."

"That's all I can ask," he replied.

Quickly, she turned from him and began gathering the dishes while he folded the quilt. Then, after one final kiss, he watched as she started for the trail through the broomsage. At the trailhead, she stopped and blew him a kiss. He blew back the kiss, then watched as her silhouette disappeared into the darkness.

June 12, 1961: Tonight, I was with Paul again. Somehow, he always takes me away from myself. I've never known a man like this!! He's such a dreamer. I love that part of him. Every time I am with him, I am taken away from myself and carried to some sort of wonderland. This man is pure magic. Never did I ever dream I would know a man like this. It is like he swallows me up in his love. He clothes me and bathes me in a robe of pure emotion that is almost unnatural. Tonight, I felt like Alice in Wonderland or Dorothy in the wizard. Oh, God what am I doing? I am so frightened by all of this!

Downtown

Over the next few weeks, Paul returned to watching and waiting. Every day, as he worked, he kept an eye on the homestead. Each time he saw her, his heart leapt with pure excitement. Whether she was hanging out clothes, working in the garden, or going to milk the cow, the very sight of her sent his spirits soaring. With each sighting, his need grew stronger. Although she was more than three hundred yards away, he could taste her lips and smell her breasts. She was so close, yet so far away.

It was the second week in July and Paul hadn't been with her for almost a month. Over the previous week, the big rig truck had been gone for three nights, but he received no messages. As he watched her go about her daily routine, she would occasionally glance briefly in his direction, but never a sign of recognition. He wondered if something was wrong.

During the last week in July, on a Saturday, Paul woke up thinking of her. The previous night, he had dreamed of being with her. He dreamed they were together as teenagers, maybe fourteen or fifteen years old in his childhood bed at his parents' home. They had folded themselves up in the old red-checkered bedcover he remembered from his childhood and joined their bodies in love again and again. As he remembered the dream, his mind harked back to Romeo and Juliet. When he awoke, he could taste her lips and smell her hair and breasts.

At breakfast with the crew the next morning, Will and Pete were arguing about a movie. Will kept saying he didn't like the ending while Pete claimed the movie couldn't end any other way. Throughout the conversation, Paul hadn't heard a word. His mind was on Cassie. After breakfast, he said good-bye to the others and went looking for her. He longed to see her. He had to be near her. He had to be in her presence whether they were going to make love or not.

Once outside, he drove to the company storage area. After he was parked, he unlocked the gate and took a vantage point in the seat of an earthmover. It was a high point and he could see the entire homestead, but an observer from the other side would never notice his vigil unless they looked closely. As he peered across the river, he could see the big rig parked in the front yard. He watched Timmy appear briefly on the back porch, then go back inside. He waited. After some thirty minutes, he saw the husband come out of the house and, fence mending tools in hand, walk along the road to the mailbox. Finally, he stopped at the fencerow and started digging a posthole. Paul watched as the husband dug the hole, placed a new post, then began tamping the earth around it. Moments later, Cassie came out of the house and fired up the old red pickup. He watched as it pulled out on the highway and headed toward Duck Springs. She was going into town. He decided to follow her.

Duck Springs was the typical south Georgia country town. Settled in the late 1890s, it had changed little over the past sixty years. On one side of the main street, some eight to ten storefronts had been jammed together side by side. Like stores in old western towns, the fronts were high and flat like highway billboards and each proclaimed the business' name. There was Glover's General Store, a drug store, a hardware company, a furniture business, and a clothing outlet. On the opposite side, there was a city hall, a post office, and a small city park. As he drove slowly down the main street, Paul knew he could have been in any one of a thousand country towns in south Georgia. This one just happened to be named Duck Springs.

Paul watched as she parked the old red pickup on the main street. When she got out, she was dressed up. Wearing a small hat and a light blue dress, she appeared quite handsome. He had never seen her dressed up before. She strode down the sidewalk and went into Glover's General Store. Moments later, Paul parked his pickup and started walking to the general store.

Once he arrived in front of the store, he peeped in the window. She was talking to the clerk. He waited. He debated whether he should go inside or wait for her to come out before accosting her. Finally, he decided to go in. Inside, the store was a replica of an old country store from the 1930s. There was an old-fashioned pot-bellied stove, a cracker barrel, a checkboard atop a nail keg, and the smell of new sawdust, which was used to clean the floor. The business stocked all of the essentials needed by the local populace. They offered groceries, feed, seed, a few dry goods, and minor farm and gardening supplies. It was Saturday morning and several shoppers were milling about. Paul could see her along the back wall of the store looking through the meat section. Moments later, she moved to the canned goods section. He appeared behind her, pretending to inspect a can of pineapple. Suddenly, she turned as she saw him.

"Are you crazy?" she whispered angrily. "What are you doing here?"

"I had to see you," he said.

"Get out of here," she whispered. "We can't be seen together."

"Now don't be too mad," he whispered innocently. "I have to shop just like you do."

She giggled, then looked around the store to see if anyone was watching. Another shopper came down the aisle. Instantly, she moved away and turned down the dry goods section. She stopped in front of some shirts. Moments later, he was behind her, pretending to be examining some underwear.

"When can I see you again?" he whispered.

She inhaled resignedly. "I don't know," she whispered. "It's going to be a while."

She didn't look at him.

"You'll have to wait for a message," she continued.

"Can we do a quickie here on the general store floor?" he whispered.

She laughed, then her laughter suddenly turned to anger. "Get away from me!" she whispered. "You're going to have to wait."

"Want some licorice?" he asked.

"I told you to get away from me."

He pretended to be looking at a dress tie. "Okay. Okay," he whispered. "I'll wait."

"Be patient," she said. "I'll leave you a message."

Quickly, he turned and started to the candy case at the front counter.

"Can I get three of those licorice sticks?" he asked.

The clerk fished three lengths of licorice out of a glass jar with tissue. He paid the clerk, then started for the door.

At the door, he turned and glanced back at her. She was watching him. Once she saw he was peering at her, she quickly turned away. Outside, he walked along the sidewalk to his truck. Inside the truck, he started chewing one of the licorice sticks and waited. Twenty minutes later, through his rear view mirror, he saw her come out of the general store with an armload of groceries. Behind her was a clerk, who was also carrying groceries. Together, they loaded the groceries into the red pickup. Moments later, he watched as she fired up the engine and turned the old red truck back toward the homestead. He was glad he had followed her. Just the sight of her, just being in her presence, meant so much to him.

* * * *

The following Monday morning, he saw the calf in the front pasture. That afternoon after work, he went to the peach tree.

I don't know when I can see you again. My husband is only working three days a week making short runs to Atlanta and back. I miss you, but I can't take a chance of my husband finding out about us. If I see that he is going to be gone for a while, I will leave you a message. Be patient with me. I haven't forgotten you. Please be patient. I miss you! Oh, God, I miss you so.

As he read the note, he was pleased. At least he now had some hope of seeing her again. When there was no communication between them, he felt helpless and alone.

Stolen Moments

It was the last week in July. Most of the week, Paul had been on a compacting machine on the west side of the river. Day after day, he would make pass after pass compressing the new base until state workers were satisfied that the soil density met compaction standards. Once state employees approved, a massive concrete laying machine would pour thousands of pounds of wet cement atop the base for the new center slabs. Earlier that month, concrete workmen had poured and finished the bridge support structures. The only work remaining on the bridges was pouring the concrete for the spans. The project was progressing well.

Day after day, as the hot summer droned on, Paul kept an eye on the homestead. For over two weeks now, Cassie had been a busy little bee. The garden was coming in and, in the mornings, decked out in her light blue pioneer bonnet, she would gather vegetables. Some mornings, he would see her on her hands and knees, picking pole beans. Other mornings, she would be standing up and moving slowly along the rows of okra, clipping the smaller, tender pods and tossing them into a dishpan. Then there was sweet corn, yellow squash, and tomatoes.

Her afternoons were spent preparing and canning the vegetables. On the back porch, in clear sight of Paul, she would sit and string and snap pole beans, then pack them into jars. Once she had ten jars, all that would fit in the old iron pressure cooker, she would go inside and get the batch started on the stove. Since she had only one pressure cooker, the canning process was much slower than the picking and packing. It had been more than a month since they had seen one another.

* * * *

On Tuesday of that week, Paul decided he was going to see her. He had an overwhelming need to be with her. Seeing her day after day only intensified his need. He wasn't sure how it would happen. He would wait for an opportunity. Wednesday and Thursday passed. On Friday morning, he had seen her in the garden, picking yellow squash, then, around lunchtime, she went back inside. Then, around 3:30 p.m., he saw the husband come out, fire up the big rig, and drive away. An hour later, she reappeared in the garden. After only thirty minutes of gathering squash, a sudden drenching rain came up and he saw her dash into the barn hallway for shelter. He couldn't work in the downpour; the big rig was gone. This was his opportunity.

Quickly, he moved the compactor to the storage area, clocked out, and, in the driving rain, made his way along the path beside the river. At the cane break, he stopped briefly, then darted through the broomsage patch. Moments later, he was standing in the barn hallway, dripping with summer rain. At the other end of the hallway, he could see her peering out into the rain, her back to him. He waited. The rain was falling steadily.

"Hello," he said finally.

Startled, she turned at the sound of his voice.

"You scared me," she said. "What are you doing here?"

"I had to see you," he said. "I'm going crazy seeing you day after day and not being able to hold you and touch you."

She was ecstatic.

"I didn't see the truck, so I came to be with you," he continued. "Even if it is just for a moment."

She smiled and looked into his eyes. His hair was wet and the fresh rain was rolling down his cheeks. She reached up and took his face lovingly in her hands.

"I'm so glad you're here," she said. "I've missed you too."

He kissed her and she returned the kiss in kind. A rush of raw desire darted through her body.

Suddenly, he pulled away.

"What's wrong?" she asked.

Gently, he removed the pioneer bonnet from her head, examined it, then placed it on his own head.

She burst out laughing at the sight of the bonnet on his head. Then he removed the bonnet and took her into his arms again.

"Come on," she said. "Let's go to the hay room."

Hand-in-hand, they raced to the end of barn hallway.

Moments later, she opened the door to the feed room. It smelled of fresh hay and dry feed for animals. Quickly, they undressed and threw their clothing on the hay for cushioning. As he thrust his body into hers, he remembered how he loved the smell of hay. The smell of the hay and the smell of an aroused woman seemed so natural together. Both were such a fresh, natural smell. Quickly, they were finished.

She lay back on the crumpled clothes.

"Oh God, I needed that," she said.

"So did I," he replied.

"You've got to go," she said. "Austin is on a short run to Savannah and will be back tonight."

"I understand," he said.

"Thanks," she said.

"Thank YOU!" he replied.

Moments later, he was darting back through the rain along the river path. He was soaking wet when he arrived at his truck, but it had been worth it. He was so relaxed and at peace with himself after being with her.

July 24, 1961: Paul is so special. With Austin, there are no surprises. He is always the same. He dresses the same, acts the same, does the same thing over and over, day after day. He is what he is and will remain so for his entire life. Paul, on the other hand, is full of surprises. I am always discovering something different and new about him. I never know what new thing I'm going to discover next. I love to be around this man. Every time I see him, I can't wait to be with him again. He brings out feelings of desire that I didn't even know I had.

* * * *

It was the first week of August and Paul was desperate for another chance to be with her. The only time he felt he had an opportunity was when she was at the barn. All he needed was just a small window. Just thirty or forty minutes to be with her. Finally, he decided to meet her while she was milking. During the spring, when they first met, she had been milking around 4:30 in the afternoon. Now that she was busy canning, the time had been pushed up and she had been milking the cow after he got off work.

On Thursday of that week, he saw the big rig was gone. After he clocked out, he decided to loiter with the crew at the storage area and wait until she went to milk. Paul knew she had to milk the cow at some point. His country upbringing had taught him a cow should be milked every day.

As he waited, Will and the crew were talking about the progress on the job.

"Mr. Gartman is very happy with the project," Will said. "We're way ahead of schedule. Paving will start next week. If the weather holds and we don't have any breakdowns, we could be finished two months early."

As Will spoke, Paul glanced across the pasture. He saw Cassie, milk bucket in hand, striding across the backyard.

He turned to the others.

"Okay, guys," he said. "I'll see you tomorrow."

Quickly, he made his way along the river trail to the cane break, then to the barn. He glanced into the hallway. She was on a milking stool, her back to him.

He coughed.

She turned.

"It's you again!" she said.

"Who else did you expect?"

She laughed.

For a long moment, he stood behind her, watching her milk the cow. He watched as she squeezed and pulled the cow's front teats and the stream of fresh, warm milk made a squishing sound as it struck the bottom of the tin bucket.

"I've missed you," he said, stroking her bare arms with his hands. "I've missed you so."

At his touch, she felt a shiver of desire dart through her body.

"I've always wanted to watch you milk the cow," he said, speaking softly and licking her neck.

Somehow, she was afraid to give in to his advances on such short notice. Despite this, his touch was feeding her need.

"Don't! Don't! Don't do that!" she said, wiggling her shoulders to make him stop.

She dipped her fingers in the warm milk and flicked it playfully behind her. He could taste the warm whole milk on his tongue. He nibbled at her ears.

"Now don't do that," she said again. "I've got to get this cow milked."

"I can't wait," he said.

"You're crazy!" she said.

For a long moment, she gave in to the signals her body was sending. As he licked her ears, she could feel the warmth rising between her legs. Then, she knew she could resist no longer. She stopped milking.

"Oh, God! Oh God," she said. "Touch my breasts!"

Still standing behind her, he unbuttoned the top of her shirt and slipped his hands gently over her breasts, cupping each one with his strong, lean hands and began slowly massaging her nipples with his thumbs.

For a moment, he could feel her body tense, then jerk forward.

"Ooooooh," she moaned, feeling a rush of sensual pleasure shoot violently throughout her body. She could feel her muscles tighten and her entire body suddenly convulsed with the wave of sensations. Finally, her entire face screwed up in a tight grimace, her body jerked forward, and she let out a loud scream.

Still sitting on the milking stool and breathing hard, she leaned forward, her head resting on the side of the cow.

"Are you okay?" he asked, removing his hands.

"I'm fine," she said. "Give me just a moment."

Suddenly, from the house, she heard Timmy's voice.

"Mommy! Mommy!!"

"That's Timmy!" she said, genuine fright in her eyes. "You've got to leave."

She stood up quickly, readjusted her brassiere, and re-buttoned the top of the dress.

"Go!" she said, pointing to the barn hallway. "Go! Go!"

Instantly, he was through the door and disappeared into the field of tall broomsage.

Once he was gone, milk bucket in hand, she walked to the end of the barn hallway. Timmy was standing on the back porch, crying.

"Timmy?" she called.

"Mommy, are you okay?"

"I'm fine, baby," she said. "Let me finish milking and I'll be right there."

July 30, 1961: I've got to be very careful. Today, when I went to Timmy, he asked me why I screamed. I told him a bat had flown out of the barn and scared me. He knows how afraid I am of bats. I only pray that he doesn't mention it to his father. That was close. I'll have to be very careful in the future.

August Heat

It was late August. Day after day, the south Georgia sun beat down with a relentless vengeance. Most days were in the high nineties and sometimes temperatures soared well over one hundred degrees. Paul was working on the east side of the river on an earthmover, dredging up topsoil to finish the shoulders. Meanwhile, the paving machines were going full bore laying asphalt. Hour after hour, dump trucks one after another dumped their load of tar-smelling asphalt into the paving machines. August was the perfect month for paving because the extreme heat allowed the tar to cure slower and provide a harder top layer for the new highway. So the paving crew would have free access to work, the old two-lane highway had been converted to a single lane. On either side of the paving operation, orange barricade cones lined the edges of the lanes and flagmen with walkie-talkies and signs controlled all incoming and outgoing traffic.

For Cassie, late August meant it was time to start canning peaches. Along the fencerow at the back pasture, the peach trees were heavy with ripe fruit. Each morning would be spent picking peaches and, once she had picked a bushel basket full, she would lug it to the back porch. There in clear sight of Paul, she would sit in the porch swing and spend the afternoon peeling, packing, and canning peaches.

On Monday of that week, she was in the middle of the latest round. On the table in front of her, she had peeled and packed twenty quarts. That was two loads for the pressure cooker. She dropped a sprinkle of seasoning into each jar and tightened the lid. Then, five at a time, she carried them into the kitchen, placed them in the pressure cooker, and turned heat on the unit.

When she returned to the back porch to start peeling peaches again, she peered across the pasture. On the other side of the highway, she could see Paul bouncing up and down on the seat of the earthmover. Again and again, she watched as he made pass after pass across the hillside, scooping up giant bites of topsoil, then unloading it in a central pile for the dump trucks. His shirt was off and the blistering sun reflected off his tanned shoulders and back. He was wearing a hat and, while she couldn't see it, she knew the brim would be wet with his sweat. August dust devils swirled around the machine and she knew the dust, mixed with his body sweat, was forming a film of grit on his arms and shoulders.

As she watched him, she could feel her need rising. She knew every inch and crevice of his body. The hairs on his chest, his muscular upper body, and the gentle fall of his neck into his shoulders. She knew only too well the faint body odor he always had, even after showering and using deodorant. At the memory of that smell, she could feel herself moisten. *It's this August heat,* she thought. *It's driving me mad with desire.* In her mind, she imagined herself lying naked with him on the old quilt in the moonlight. With the thought, she felt this savage passion welling up within her. *I'm going to have this man as soon as I can,* she told herself. *I need him.*

* * * *

On Thursday of that week, Austin announced he was going to his mother's the following Saturday afternoon and would return around ten p.m. the same night. This was her chance. On Friday morning, she put the calf in the front and went to the far peach tree.

The note read:

Saturday night. 8 p.m. At the cane break.

When they met two nights later, she only brought the quilt.

"I can't stay here long," she said. "My husband will be back in a few hours."

"I'm just glad to be with you," he said. "I've missed you so."

For more than thirty minutes, they were like two wild animals clawing at one another. They were two raging bodies of flesh tearing at the body of the other. Finally, their passions spent, they rested on the old quilt.

"Are you happy now?" she asked.

"Oh yes!" he replied. "Are you?"

"Very happy," she replied. "I always enjoy you so much." She stood up. "I've got to go now," she said.

He stood up. "When will I see you again?"

"I'm not sure," she said. "Next week, Austin starts making short trips to Atlanta again, so he will be home most nights."

His face took on a disgusted look.

"Now don't be getting all droopy faced," she said. "I haven't forgotten you. It's just that it's going to be a while."

"I understand," he said. "Can I get one more kiss?"

She went to him. Their lips met, then she turned and started up the trail through the broomsage. Suddenly, she stopped.

"Be patient with me," she said. "Okay?"

"Okay," he said.

She blew him a kiss, then disappeared up the trail.

* * * *

The following night, after dinner at the motel restaurant, Paul and the Gartman crew were in the motel bar drinking beer and playing pool. Paul had been playing doubles with Joanne, a slim brunette and regular patron he had met at the bar.

"We won five straight games," she said, taking a seat at the Gartman table. "We make a pretty good team."

"Yes, we do," Paul said, taking a seat beside her. "Want to play again?"

She peered at him, a mischievous glint in her eye.

"I would rather go back to my room and show you my embroidery collection," she said.

"Do you embroider?" Paul asked.

"Oh, yes," she said, putting her hand on his knee. "I have some very nice pieces I could show you."

Paul smiled.

She waited.

"Come on, Paul," she said. "What do you say?"

She waited again.

"I appreciate the invite," Paul said finally. "But I'm having lots of fun here with my buddies tonight." Paul could see she was miffed at his reply. "Besides, I've got to get up early tomorrow for work."

She peered at him. "You're sure?" she said. "I only offer once."

"I'm sure," Paul replied.

She stood up. "You don't know what you're missing," she said.

"Thanks anyway," he said.

Quickly, the woman turned and started to the bar.

The other members of the Gartman crew watched the woman's hips as she strode to the bar.

"Paul, what's going on with you?" Knox said. "I've seen the day when you'd be all over an offer like that."

Paul smiled sheepishly. "I guess times change," he said. "I'm getting older now."

The other crewmembers laughed.

"You sure it hasn't got anything to do with that little blonde over at the homestead?" Knox asked.

Paul looked up at Knox. Anger flashed across his face. "Leave her out of this!" he said.

Knox drew back. He could see the anger in Paul's eyes. "You don't have to act like that," Knox said. "I was only kidding. I didn't mean to offend you."

"You didn't offend me," Paul said, "Just mind your own business."

The crewmembers looked from one to the other.

The table grew quiet.

Will saw an opportunity to break the icy silence. "Well, I think I've had enough tonight," Will said. "We got a big day ahead of us tomorrow. I'm going to turn in."

"I'm leaving too," Paul said. He stood up from the table. "Good night, fellows," Paul said.

The others said goodnight.

Moments later, Paul and Will had paid their bar bills and were walking across the parking lot.

"Those guys aren't blind," Will said. "All of them know you've been messing around with that blonde over at the homestead."

"Maybe I took it the wrong way," Paul said.

"Yeah," Will replied. "You REALLY took it the wrong way."

"Sometimes, I just wish those guys would mind their own business."

"They didn't mean anything," Will said. "They were just kidding."

Making Plans

It would be over two months before they would see one another again. Throughout the remainder of September and October, the truck was at the house every night. On September 22, the autumn equinox, Paul was about to give up hope. She was on his mind constantly and, every night, he longed to be with her. He missed running his fingers along the arch of her neck down to her shoulders. He missed seeing the wildfire in her eyes when she was aroused. It was the smell of her breasts he missed the most. The smell, the taste of her breasts was something magical to him. It was a pure, raw scent, like a mild body odor, but it was faintly sweet like a young honeysuckle blossom in springtime. Sometimes, in his dreams, he would imagine he was with her and, after he woke up, he could still smell that natural womanly scent of her breasts.

Although he longed for her with every fabric of his being, there was nothing he could do but watch and wait. He kept reassuring himself that she would contact him when she could get away. The month of October passed with no communications. Then, on November second, the calf was in the front pasture.

The note read:

Thursday night. 8:30. In the hayroom.

The night was pitch black when he parked his truck at the company storage area. Using a flashlight, he made his way along the path beside the river to the cane break, then went up the path through the broomsage. She was waiting in the barn hallway. Inside the hay room, she had spread the old quilt across a nest of soft hay and an old kerosene lantern provided light. Their lovemaking was fast and furious. Once finished, she turned to him.

"I have some news," she said.

"What's that?"

"Austin's mother called today," she said. "She wants me and Timmy to come visit them for Thanksgiving."

"Are you going?"

"No," she replied. "I told them I have to take care of a sick calf and couldn't leave."

"So...?"

"They said they would come get him. I'll be alone for two days."

He looked at her.

"Two days?"

She nodded.

"What about your husband?"

"He's leaving on the twentieth for Oregon. He'll be gone for over a week."

He continued to look at her. "You mean we could have two whole days together?"

She nodded again.

"You want to go to Atlanta?"

She smiled. "Do you think we could do it and nobody find out about it?"

"Who's going to know?" he asked. "When are they coming to get Timmy?"

"Around noon on Wednesday and they'll bring him back Friday afternoon."

"That means we could have Wednesday night and Thursday night together," he said.

She was still hesitant. "Do you think it would be okay?"

"Like I said, who would ever know?"

"Can we visit Margaret Mitchell's home?" she asked.

"Sure," he replied. "We could go to Little Five Points and see all the crazies. We could eat at a fancy restaurant. We could go shopping. We could even go see a movie."

"Oh, I would love that," she said. "There's something else I want to do."

"What's that?"

"Now don't laugh when I tell you."

"I'm not going to laugh," he said. "Tell me."

"I want to ride in a taxi."

He laughed.

"You promised not to laugh."

He was still giggling at the thought. "I'm sorry," he said. "You've never ridden in a taxi?"

"How am I going to ride in a taxi?" she said. "I'm just a country girl living out here in the wilds of south Georgia. When am I ever going to ride in a taxi?"

"Okay! Okay!" he said. "We'll ride in a taxi. So what time?"

"It's according to when they come to get Timmy," she said. "Shouldn't be any later than noon on Wednesday."

"That's perfect," he said. "I get off at noon on Wednesday. I'll be waiting at the cane break around 12:30."

She peered into his eyes. Like a little girl, she was giddy with excitement.

"Oh, Paul, I can't wait."

"It will be something we'll always remember."

She turned her face to him for a kiss.

He kissed her lightly on the lips.

Moments later, they were dressed. After a last kiss, she turned and headed back up the path through the broomsage.

As he watched her disappear back along the path, he told himself this was his Annabel Lee. This was the woman he had been waiting for all these years. All of the deep-seated passion he had been lugging around waiting to give to some woman, he was going to give to Cassie. He was going to pour all of his emotions and passions totally and completely into her. He was going to drown himself. Even if she was married, he didn't care. He would soon be forty and this was probably his last chance. Whatever the consequences, he would deal with it. It was now or never.

Going to Atlanta

At noon on Wednesday, the day before Thanksgiving, Paul parked his machine in the storage area, clocked out, and left work. Back at the motel, he packed a suitcase with two days of clothes, toilet gear, and some comfortable shoes for walking. At his truck, he threw the suitcase in the front seat and slid under the steering wheel. Before starting the engine, he opened the console to check for his pistol. The .38 special was there. Any time he was going on a long trip, he made sure he had his pistol. Once, when he first began working for Gartman, he was on a job in Sylacauga, Alabama when he was robbed. Late one night, he had left a bar and was going to his truck. As he unlocked the door, a black man approached, pushed a pistol into his back, and demanded his billfold. It crossed his mind to resist, but his better judgment told him he shouldn't, so he gave the robber his billfold. The following day, he bought the pistol. Next time, he would have some protection. Since then, he always kept a pistol in the truck glove compartment.

Twenty minutes later, he parked his truck at the company storage area, then crossed the highway and scrambled down the embankment to the river trail. Moments later, as he approached the cane break, he saw her waiting, suitcase in hand.

He went to her and embraced her.

"I love you," he said.

"I love you too," she replied.

Thirty minutes later, they were in his truck, cruising north to Atlanta.

"This is the first time we've really had a chance to relax and talk to one another," he said.

"I know," she said. "Let's make the most of it."

* * * *

Along the highway to Atlanta, scattered billboards announced the businesses ahead of them. There were advertisements for restaurants, hotels, Burma Shave, service stations, clothing stores, local produce, fresh pecans, and divinity candy.

"Can we stop and buy some divinity?" she asked.

"Sure," he said. "We'll get some when we stop for gas."

They rode quietly for some fifteen minutes, taking in the sights along the road and listening to Roy Orbison on the radio singing "Crying."

Finally, she spoke. "Don't you ever get tired of bouncing up and down on those road machines all day?"

"I love my job," he said. "I love traveling and building highways. It's my life."

She didn't answer immediately.

"What about you?" he asked. "Don't you ever get tired of staying on that farm day after day?"

"Yes, I do get tired sometimes," she said. "But I don't really have a choice."

"What do you mean?"

"I'm twenty-seven years old and God has put me in the place I will be for the rest of my life. I am bound to spend the rest of my life married to Austin and taking care of Timmy. I'll devote myself to him until he dies."

Paul was startled at her words.

"Until he dies?"

"Yes," she replied. "Doctors say people with the disease he has usually die when they're in their early twenties."

"What's wrong with him?" he asked.

"Doctors have a name for it," she said. "They call it microencephaly. When he was born, his brain was smaller than normal. That's what causes him to have fits. It's something in Austin's family."

Paul shook his head sadly. "I'm sorry to hear that," Paul said. "I know what it's like to be a disabled child."

She was shocked to hear the words. "What?" she said. "What would you know about being disabled?"

"I haven't always been as strong and healthy as I am now," he said. "When I was eight years old and in the second grade, I had polio. My parents took me out of school and, for three years, I had to wear braces and use crutches until I regained the strength in my legs. I know what it's like to be called crippled and have to depend on other people to help you do the simplest things."

"You quit going to school?"

"Not exactly," he said. "My mother home schooled me those three years. She was trained to be a schoolteacher. I went back to regular school when I was twelve, but I'll never forgot those three years. Being disabled like that teaches you to be humble and understanding of others who have disabilities."

She studied him. "You were very close to your mother, weren't you?" she asked.

He nodded.

"Yes, very close," he replied. "That's why it almost killed me when she died."

"Is that where you got your soft, sensitive side?"

He nodded. "Yeah," he said. "Sometimes, I'm too sensitive."

She smiled. "That's the side I love about you," she said. "Your soft gentle side that is not afraid to show your feelings. Most men I have known in my life are afraid to show their feelings. They have to always be tough and manly. They think showing feelings is a sign of weakness."

"Yes, I have a soft side," he replied, "but I'm very masculine at the same time."

She laughed. "Yes, I know," she said, reaching over and placing her hand on his thigh. "Do you have to remind me?"

He laughed. They rode quietly.

"Like I said," he said finally. "I wish there was something I could do to help you with your son."

"Do you really mean that?"

"Yes," he said. "I would do anything for you."

She was silent for a moment. "Have you ever thought about having children of your own?"

"Oh yes," he said. "I would love to have a son and watch him grow up and teach him things."

She didn't answer.

"I just never met the woman I wanted to marry and have a child with."

"Have you ever been in love?"

He smiled. "Yes," he said. "One time. Once, when I was working on a job in Duck Springs, Georgia, I fell in love with this beautiful woman. She was a small blonde with a nice smile, a wonderful body, and her breasts smelled like honeysuckle in springtime."

She giggled with delight. "You're talking about me!"

"Yes, I'm talking about you," he said. "I've fallen madly in love with you. I would do anything for you."

"Do you really, really mean that?"

"Why do you keep asking me that?"

"You keep forgetting that I'm a married woman."

"Yes, I do," he said.

"Why?"

"Because I've never known a woman like you," he said. "I'm not going to miss the chance, even if you're married."

She peered out the window.

They rode quietly.

"You don't have the same feelings for me?" he asked.

She was quiet.

"I have to admit," she said finally, "there are lots of things I like about you...."

She lingered.

"I like your craziness," she continued. "You make me laugh. I like you because you're full of surprises. I like your soft side. I like the silly things you do. I like the fact that I can talk to you about anything...."

She stopped and started laughing.

"Why are you laughing?"

"I'll always remember the night when we were playing Adam and Eve and you started carrying on about our Garden of Eden. I'll remember that until the day I die."

He smiled.

"Most of all, I love being with you as a woman," she said. "You've brought out a whole new side to my passions. You've taken me to places in my body I never even dreamed I had."

He didn't respond.

"Now that I stop to think of it, there are lots of things I like about you," she continued. "And you've grown in my heart like a vine growing up the trunk of a tree."

They rode quietly.

"Yes," she said finally. "I think I've fallen in love with you too."

"Do you really mean that?"

"Yes," she said. "I really mean it."

They rode quietly. Bored, Paul turned on the radio. Bobby Lewis was singing "Tossing and Turning." For several minutes, Paul hummed along with the tune, then he saw a gas station sign ahead advertising pecan divinity.

"We'll stop at the next exit," he said. "I'll get gas and you can buy some divinity."

Twenty minutes later, with a full tank of gas and a sackful of divinity, they were back on the road. They rode quietly, listening to Del Shannon singing "Runaway" and munching on the divinity.

Finally, she spoke. "Would you really do anything for me?" she asked.

"That's the fourth time you've asked me that," he said. "What are you getting at?"

She lingered with her answer. "I'm not sure I know how to say this," she said.

"Say it anyway."

"Would you give me your child?" she asked.

Suddenly, he felt an explosion in his mind. That was the last thing he had expected to hear. "You want to have a child with me?"

"Yes," she said. "I want to have another child, but not with my husband."

She waited for the words to register.

"I don't want to have another child that has the same affliction Timmy has," she said. "I want a child who is healthy and happy and can grow up to be normal."

He didn't answer.

She waited. "You don't want to give me your child?" she asked.

They rode quietly. Finally, he spoke. "If we had a child and you were with your husband, I would never see it or get to enjoy it."

"That's true," she said. "But you wouldn't have to worry about it. I would take care of the child and love it and always be a good mother to it."

He looked at her.

"I want to have some way to remember you," she said.

He didn't answer.

"Will you do that for me?" she asked.

"Yes," he replied. "If that's what you want...."

"I'm very fertile right now," she said. "No protection for the next two nights... Okay?"

"Okay," he said.

They rode quietly. Outside the car window, the fallow cotton fields and pecan orchards of south Georgia were rolling past. On the radio, Patsy Cline was singing "I Fall to Pieces."

"Want some more divinity?" Cassie asked finally.

"No," Paul replied. "I've had enough."

Cassie rolled up the top of the sack and put it in her purse.

"Can I ask you a question?" he said.

"Sure."

"Do you ever have relations with your husband?"

"Do you really want to know the answer to that?"

"I wouldn't have asked if I didn't want to know."

She lingered with the answer. "We have relations once, maybe twice a month, but it's not anything to enjoy. It's over in a couple minutes. Making love is a chore to Austin. Like taking out the garbage or going to the mail box."

"Don't you hate that?"

"Of course," she said. "That's why I'm with you. I'm a natural born woman and I need a man."

"Why don't you leave him?"

"Oh, I could never take Timmy away from his daddy," she replied. "He thinks his father is God. Already he plans to be a long-haul truck driver like his father. He wants toy trucks for Christmas and birthdays."

"I thought you said he wouldn't live past the age of twenty."

"He won't," Cassie replied. "What am I supposed to do? Tell my son he can never grow up to be a truck driver like his father because he won't live past the age of twenty?"

Paul took a deep breath. "I see what you mean," he said. "I'm sorry."

"No reason to be sorry," she said. "It is what it is."

They rode quietly.

"Well, I'm glad your husband is a terrible lover," Paul said finally. "That means I have you all to myself."

She turned to him.

"Can we talk about something else?"

Atlanta

It was almost five p.m. when they arrived in Atlanta. Near midtown, Paul rented a room at the Jefferson Davis Inn. Over the years, he had stayed there during his treks between the company's headquarters in Nashville and his father's home in Florida. It was just off the main highway, the rooms were clean and quiet, and the television reception was tolerable. Once he had paid the clerk, he drove his truck to the room and, suitcases in hand, they got out. He unlocked the door.

"Look at this!" she said, setting down her suitcase and flopping on the king-size bed. "We've got a real bed tonight."

"We're moving up in the world," he said.

"Think our lovemaking will be better on a real bed?"

He laughed. "When we're going at one another," he said, "we pay no attention to what is under us."

She laughed. She knew he was right.

"What do you want to do now?" he asked.

"I'm tired after the trip," she said. "Let's eat and get a good night's sleep."

"Sounds good," he said. "We've got a big day ahead of us tomorrow."

After a dinner of kung pao chicken and steamed vegetables, they returned to the motel. That night was the first time they were able to relax together and get to know one another's bodies. There were no restraints. They weren't looking over their shoulders or fearing they would be discovered, so they let themselves go with one another. They bathed in one another. Three separate times they made love and, each and every time, she was fully satisfied as a woman.

Finally, breathing hard and hearts pounding against one another's chests, they clung to each other.

"You give me so much," she said.

"That's because I love you like I do," he replied.

Moments later, they were asleep in one another's arms.

***

It was Thursday morning, Thanksgiving Day, 1961. They had breakfast at the motel restaurant, then returned to the room to make preparations to go to Margaret Mitchell's house. Paul had an address he had copied from the phone book and, note in hand, they left the room.

Five minutes later, they were standing in front of the motel.

"I thought we were going to Margaret Mitchell's house," she said.

"We are," he replied.

"Aren't you going to take the truck?"

"No."

"How are we going to get there?"

"We're going to take a taxi."

She smiled, then she turned and kissed him.

* * * *

The Margaret Mitchell home was a turn-of-the century, three-story Tudor revival building in midtown Atlanta. Actually, it was not a home, but a reconverted apartment building where Mitchell had lived while she wrote *Gone with the Wind*. As they toured the apartment, the guide explained the author's activities in each room and noted historical mementoes relative to her personal life at the time. At the bottom of the wooden staircase on the first floor, there was a fist-sized knob atop the support column, which Mitchell supposedly ran her hand over every day for good luck. In keeping with tradition, Paul and Cassie rubbed their hands on the knob. In a separate part of the building, there was a huge display of little known facts about the production of the movie and its cast. It included the director's original storyboards, which would later depict scenes from the movie. The tour ended at a gift shop.

"Want to buy a souvenir?" Paul asked.

"We better not," she said. "I would be a single woman if my husband found something like that."

"Then let's go to Little Five for dinner and a movie."

"What's Little Five?" she asked.

"That's where all the crazies are," he replied. "All the artistic types that want to live free of money and the daily cares of regular people. They live only for their art."

"I've never seen anything like that."

* * * *

The taxi ride to Little Five Points was a visual feast for Cassie. She marveled at the skyscrapers in downtown Atlanta, the streetcars, the infinite variety of shops, and the exclusive restaurants.

"Look how tall those buildings are," she said as the taxi passed through midtown Atlanta. "I've never seen so many black folks," she said as the taxi cruised down Sweet Auburn Avenue.

In late 1961, Little Five Points, so named because it marked the convergence of five major city streets, was the hip, trendy section of Atlanta. Over the past thirty years, it had become a magnet for Bohemian-minded individuals seeking an alternative lifestyle. It had become a haven for writers, musicians, painters, and other wanna-be artists who sought to live in an enclave of like-minded people. Its streets were lined with bookstores, record shops, art galleries, music stores, arts and crafts boutiques, and coffee shops. "Little Five" was to Atlanta what Haight-Ashbury was to San Francisco or Greenwich Village to New York.

At Moreland Avenue, Paul and Cassie got out of the taxi, then, arm-in-arm, strolled along the sidewalk. There was an assortment of street entertainment, including street preachers, mom and pop musical groups, magicians, jugglers, and a contortionist.

"This is like the circus," Cassie said, giggling with childish delight. "And it's all for free."

For a moment, they stopped and watched a juggler as he kept five bowling pins in the air. Then they moved on to a street preacher and then a gospel-singing act. An older man with a flowing beard and wearing overalls played fiddle, a middle-aged man in a black cowboy hat was on guitar, and a youngish, chubby woman was singing "I'll Fly Away."

Several members of the crowd sang along, then Cassie joined in on the chorus.

"I'll fly away, oh glory, I'll fly away in the morning," she sang. "When I die, hallelujah bye and bye, I'll fly away."

When the chorus came around the second time, Cassie was singing along with the lyrics. "I'll fly away, oh glory, I'll fly away..."

Suddenly, at just the precise moment, Paul chimed in with "In the morning..." in a strong bass voice.

Instantly, upon hearing this, Cassie stopped singing and started laughing.

Moments later, after the group finished singing, Cassie was still giggling.

"You're so full of surprises," she said. "I never ever know what you're going to do next."

They moved on down the street.

Just ahead, they could see a sidewalk restaurant with a sign proclaiming "New World Coffee Shop." Seated at outside tables were ten to twelve strangely dressed young couples smoking cigarettes and sipping coffee. Most of the men had beards, some wore sunglasses and berets, and many were dressed in outlandish colors and styles. Several of the women also wore berets and dark glasses and were dressed in turtlenecks and black leotards. In front of the seating area was a small stage with a microphone and a blackboard which announced: "Open mike for poetry reading."

Cassie peered curiously at the group. "Who are these people?" she whispered.

"They are beatniks," Paul replied. "They've given up on society and making money. They want to spend their lives pursuing their art. They are angry at the world."

"They look so strange," Cassie whispered.

They watched as a young bearded man wearing sunglasses took the stage.

"What's he going to do?" Cassie asked.

"He's going to read poetry," Paul said. "Let's listen."

They watched as the man doused a cigarette and stood before the mike.

"My Death," the man said, clearing his throat and preparing to read from a sheet of paper. Behind him on the stage, a middle-aged woman wearing a beret, sunglasses, and black leotards softly played a bongo drum.

The crowd grew quiet.

With a dramatic flourish, the man raised his hand.

"There, there in the distance, I could see my death approaching. I can see his hollow eyes, his sneering grin, and his open claws ready to grasp my throat and squeeze my life away. I could feel his hot breath in my face and the leering gleam in his eye as he prepared to add my spirit to his roster of forgotten souls. I longed to escape, but I knew it would be futile. Then I felt his cold touch on my brow, his hot sweat on my face, and the essence of myself being suddenly sucked away. Then I could feel myself falling into myself and I was tumbling through the bottomless emptiness of eternity...."

There was mild applause.

The man bowed his head slightly then returned to a seat in the audience.

"He's not Edgar Allen Poe," Paul said, tugging her arm to move on.

"I've never seen people like that," Cassie said. "Don't they work and have families?"

"I don't know," Paul said.

"How do they pay their bills?" Cassie asked. "They have to have clothes and food."

Paul shrugged.

"Those are strange people," she said.

Further on, they stopped to watch another family of street singers. A middle-aged, bearded white man wearing a Mexican poncho and a sombrero was playing a harmonica and a lanky Negro woman, some ten years younger, was strumming a guitar. At their feet, a mulatto child, maybe two or three, was playing in the dirt. In front of the child was a hat for tips.

They listened as the couple sang Wood Guthrie's "This Land is Your Land." Among the crowd, some sang while others kept time with their hands. Once the song was finished, there was a round of applause and several listeners stepped forward to drop change in the hat.

Paul fished a quarter out of his pocket.

"Can I put the money in?" Cassie asked.

He handed her the quarter.

Cassie stepped forward and knelt in front of the child to place the quarter in the hat. As she did, the child looked into her eyes. For a long moment, they peered into one another's eyes. The child smiled; Cassie smiled back.

Then she returned to Paul's side and they continued down the street.

"Why did you want to do that?"

"I wanted to look into that little girl's eyes."

"What did you see?"

"I have never seen such peace and happiness in a child's face," she said.

They passed another street preacher, an art exhibit featuring paintings of nude women in various poses with outlandishly big breasts and hips. There was an elderly woman selling pieces of crochet, an Indian-looking woman selling clay pots, and a street side jeweler.

Moments later, they came upon a crowd of black people gathered around a stage where a middle-aged Negro man with salt-and-pepper hair and dressed in a business suit was preaching. Behind him, high above the stage, a sign read: "We Want Our Freedom!!" At his side and behind him, several young black men with shaved heads, fierce looks, and arms folded defiantly appeared to be the preacher's protectors.

With broad flourishes and waving a Bible, the preacher was urging the audience of mostly black people to take action.

"Now the white man is going to tell you that Negroes are inferior, that they are lazy and can't learn and all they're good for is to pick cotton and eat watermelon," the preacher was saying.

This drew a ripple of laughter from some members.

"I'm here to tell you that black people have been trod upon long enough. Unless we stand up and fight for our rights, none of this is never going to change. In twenty years, we'll be right where we are today, begging white people to give us jobs, allow us to vote, and letting us use their bathrooms..."

Several members of the crowd shouted, "Amen."

"As for me, I'm sick and tired of laughing when it ain't funny and scratching when it don't itch."

Cassie turned to Paul.

"I don't like this," she said. "Come on; let's go. I'm afraid."

* * * *

It was late afternoon. Only a small sliver of sun could be seen in the western sky. They had been strolling for almost four hours.

"Are you getting hungry?" Paul asked.

"Yes," she said. "I could eat something."

Paul pointed across the street. "There's a nice restaurant," he said. "Let go check it out."

Moments later, they stood in front of an exclusive restaurant.

"Come on," Paul said. "Let's go in here."

Cassie peeked inside. The waiters were wearing black ties and vests; men patrons were dressed in suits and wearing dinner jackets and the women were in evening attire.

"We can't go in there," she said. "Those are city people. They're wearing suits and ties."

"So?" he said. "They put on their pants just like we do, one leg at a time."

"Look at the way we're dressed," she said. "You in khakis and me in a home-made dress."

"It's clean," he said. "Come on!"

"Oh no," she said. "I can't go in a place like this. I'm a simple country woman. I wouldn't know how to act around people like that."

Paul laughed out loud. "We may never have another chance."

"You're probably right," she said. "But I can't do it."

Frustrated, he looked at her. "So what do you want to do?"

She looked down the street and her eye caught an old white woman, a shawl over her shoulders, standing over an open-fire grill, flipping hamburger patties at a street stand.

"There's where I want to go," she said.

Paul looked at her thoughtfully. "Now I know why I love you like I do," he said. "You have no pretentions or airs about you. There is no hypocrisy."

Moments later, they were standing in front of the old woman, selecting condiments for their burgers.

"Mustard and lots of pickles on mine," Cassie said.

"Same here," Paul added.

Once the sandwiches were prepared, they took a seat at a small table in front of the stand.

"We saw everything that woman did to prepare our food," Cassie said. "You never know what they're doing to your food in a fancy restaurant like that."

"As long as you're happy," he said. "That's what matters."

Once the burgers were finished, Paul dumped the aftermath into a trashcan and turned to her.

"Let's see a movie," he said.

After walking several blocks, they stopped in front of a movie theater. Two movies, *The Guns of Navarone* and *The Misfits,* were playing.

"Which do you want to see?" Paul asked. "The *Guns of Navarone* is a war adventure movie. I like Gregory Peck."

She peered at the movie broadsheets. "If that's what you want," she said.

"There are going to be lots of explosions and killing," he said.

"Yeah," she said, still reading the broadsheets. "That'll be okay."

Paul turned and joined the line to buy a ticket

"No, wait!" she said. "I want to see *The Misfits*. It's got Clark Gable."

He studied her.

"You sure do change your mind a lot."

"I have the right to change my mind," she replied. "I'm a woman."

Paul laughed, then joined the other ticket line.

The Misfits was the story of an aging cowboy played by Clark Gable and a recently divorced blonde bombshell played by Marilyn Monroe. To raise money, the cowboy and his partner decide to capture wild horses in the Nevada desert and sell them to dog food manufacturers. When the woman learns this, she pleads for the men to release the horses, especially a beautiful white stallion. After they refuse, she offers to pay them to release the horses. Finally, after a series of arguments with the cowboy, his partner, and the woman, the horses are finally released and the woman is pleased to see the white stallion running free again.

It was almost nine p.m. when they emerged from the movie. Outside, a misting rain was falling. For a moment, they waited under the shelter of the marquee.

"Come on; let's walk in the rain," he said.

"We'll get wet," she said.

"That's the whole purpose."

She laughed, then, arm-in-arm, they strolled up the street. She raised her face to the tiny raindrops and enjoyed their gentle splashing against her cheeks and face. She ran her fingers through her hair, feeling the slight wetness on her fingers. She felt so wonderful being at Paul's side.

As they walked, she knew tonight was going to be one of the most important nights of her life and she wanted to do something to make it special. They passed several shops. There was a dress shop, a vacuum cleaner outlet, a restaurant, and a clothing store. Ahead, Cassie could see a sign that read: "Claudine's Love Shop." Once they arrived, she stopped and peered in the window.

"I want to go in here," she said.

"What are you going to buy?"

"Some things for us," she said. "I want tonight to be very special."

Inside, she bought several items. On the street again, Paul hailed a taxi and, twenty minutes later, they were back at the motel.

Once inside the room, she opened the package. There was a scarlet red negligee, some scented candles, and a bottle of perfume.

"I'll take my shower first," she said. "Then I'll get ready for you."

Moments later, she was in the shower. She loved showers. At home, all she had was a bathtub, which prevented her from feeling the full fresh warmth of the water streaming over her entire body. She indulged herself in the shower, making sure she lathered every part of her body in its luxuriating warmth. Once showered, she stepped briefly out of the stall, took Paul's razor from the vanity, and returned. She wanted to be totally clean and well groomed for him tonight.

As she shaved her legs, her mind suddenly flashed on a conversation she had with her sister Audrey more than nine years earlier. Two days before Cassie was married, Audrey had sat down with her to have a sister-to-sister talk about sex. At the time, her sister had been married four years and had two children. Cassie considered her sister an expert.

"Most times," the sister had said, "if you keep herself closed up inside and your husband is using protection, you'll never get pregnant. When you're ready to take a child, you should be wide open inside and wrap your legs around your husband's waist so you can receive the full thrust of his seeds."

As she finished shaving her legs, she wondered why that thought had popped into her mind.

After a few minutes, she stepped out of the bathroom.

"Your turn," she said.

Moments later, Paul was in the bathroom, taking his shower. When he emerged fifteen minutes later, the room was dark. Several candles provided illumination. He could see her sitting on the bed wearing the negligee and holding the bottle of perfume. *She is such a beautiful woman*, he thought.

"I love the perfume," he said.

"Come sit on the bed for me," she said.

Obediently, he took a seat beside her. As he sat on the bed, she took a dab of perfume on her finger and dabbed a portion on his chin, then his right shoulder, then crossed to his left shoulder, and then his navel.

"What are you doing?"

"I want to do this with God's blessing," she said.

She looked into his eyes and kissed him.

"Now do the same thing for me," she said.

Taking the bottle of perfume, he dabbed a bit on her chin, then made a crossing motion from her right shoulder to her left shoulder, then to her navel.

"Now kiss me," she said.

He kissed her lightly on the lips.

Then she took the bottle of perfume, replaced the top, and sat it on the bedside table.

"Now I'm ready for you," she said. "I'm ready to take your child."

She lay back on the bed and beckoned him to bring his body to hers. Once he penetrated her, she wrapped her legs around his waist and locked her body to his by intertwining her feet behind him. As he thrust his body into hers again and again, she opened up the furthermost reaches of her womanhood to receive him. Finally, the rising floodtide of sensations reached a crescendo and exploded within her. At the explosion, her back arched sharply and she screamed. It was the primal, ageless scream of a woman who was being impregnated.

Moments later, breathing hard and smelling of raw sex, they lay in one another's arms.

"I love you," she said.

"I love you too," he replied.

Trip Home

The following morning, they were up early, had their showers, and were packed for the return trip to Duck Springs. When Paul started to the truck with their suitcases, he saw the bottle of perfume and the negligee on the bed.

"Aren't you going to take those?"

"I can't," she said. "If my husband saw something like either of those, I would be a single woman."

He looked at her.

"I understand," he said. "Let's go."

* * * *

An hour later, they were cruising south toward Duck Springs. For Paul, the weekend had been a magical experience and he was in good spirits.

"Want to stop for some more divinity?" he asked.

"No," she replied.

Paul looked at her. She didn't return the glance. He could feel her isolation. He could see the weepiness.

"Going to be a beautiful day," he said.

She didn't reply.

They rode quietly. Outside the truck window, the south Georgia countryside rolled past. Fallow winter fields and mile after mile of fenced pastures with grazing cattle streamed along either side of the highway. Bundles of baled hay, pecan orchards, and an occasional dairy barn dotted the roadside. Crop irrigators, which would water the cotton and soybean crops next season, stood quiet and idle. Beyond the fields, stretching to the horizon, the winter trees stood naked in their isolation.

"Are you ready for breakfast?" he asked finally.

"Suit yourself," she said.

"Are you mad at me?"

"Why would you ask that?"

"Because you're so quiet."

"I'm just sad," she said.

"Why?"

She didn't answer.

"Come on," he said. "What's eating at you?"

She looked at him.

"I'm thinking," she said finally.

"Well, I'm getting hungry," he said. "I'm going to stop in Macon and get some breakfast."

"That's fine," she said.

Just outside of Macon, they stopped at a small country restaurant for breakfast. Paul had scrambled eggs and bacon with toast and coffee. Cassie ordered oatmeal, fresh fruit, and coffee.

As she ate, Paul suddenly saw huge tears rolling down her cheeks.

"Why are you crying?" he asked.

She didn't answer at first.

"I wanted to say thanks for last night," she said.

"That's why you're crying?"

"I'm just so sad."

"Why?"

She shook her head sadly. "Come on," she said. "I'm ready to go."

"You haven't finished your meal."

Suddenly, she arose from the table and started out.

"Wait!" he said. "What's wrong?" Paul paid the check and followed her out to the truck. "Why are you acting like this?" he asked, starting the truck engine.

"Just give me a minute to calm myself," she said.

Back on the road, they rode quietly.

Finally, she spoke.

"When will your job be finished?"

"Why would you ask me that?"

"Because I need to know," she said.

He disliked the direction of the conversation.

"Probably January or February," he said finally.

"That's three months," she said. "You'll be going away." She turned to see his response.

He nodded without looking at her.

"And I'll be alone again."

He was afraid to answer.

"What's going to happen to us?" she asked.

"I'm not sure," he replied.

They rode quietly.

"You know, this has to end at some point," she said.

He shook his head in frustration. "Can't we just enjoy our time together and cross that bridge when we get to it?"

"You keep forgetting I'm a married woman."

"Why are you always so negative?"

"That's not being negative," she said. "That's being real. You've always got your head in the clouds. I like to keep my feet on the ground."

They rode quietly for some twenty minutes.

"I feel so far away from you," she said finally.

"Why?" he asked. "Don't you love me anymore?"

She took a deep breath. "Yes, I love you," she said. "I love you in a way I never dreamed I could love a man, but you know this has to end."

"That's not true," he said. "You could get a divorce from your husband and we could be married. I could adopt Timmy as my son. That's how much I love you."

"That kind of talk is silly," she said. "You're a free bird. You're like the wild stallion in that movie last night; you have to be free at all costs."

He knew she was right, but he desperately wished she was wrong.

* * * *

Two hours later, they stopped for gas and food. At a small roadside stand, they ordered barbecue, fries, and cole slaw and took a seat at an outside table. Sitting side by side, he unwrapped the sandwiches and squeezed out several packets of ketchup for her fries. Then he began to eat.

She looked at the food, then suddenly, began sobbing.

He shook his head helplessly. "Cassie," he said. "What's wrong? Every time we sit down to eat, you start crying."

"I can't bear the thought of you going away," she said. "I think I will just die when you're gone."

"Baby, it will be all right," he said. "Our lives will go on."

Huge tears were rolling down her cheeks. Sitting beside him, she turned and put her arms around him. "Hold me!" she said.

He set aside his sandwich and took her into his arms. She buried her face in his chest and sobbed uncontrollably. For several minutes, he rocked her slowly as she sobbed into his chest.

"Baby! Baby!" he said, trying to console her. "It's going to be all right. Everything is going to be just fine."

She raised her face to his. "How can you say that?" she asked. "We've fallen in love and now we've got to go our separate ways."

He looked away, shaking his head slowly in frustration. Again, she buried her face in his chest and sobbed. All the while, he continued to rock her slowly in his arms.

"Baby! Baby! Please stop crying," he said over and over.

Finally, she pulled away and wiped her eyes. "Now I feel better," she said. "Come on; let's go to Duck Springs."

"Will you stop crying?" he asked.

"Yes," she said. "I'll stop crying. I promise."

An hour later, they were cruising south to Duck Springs again. Her mood was much brighter.

"I'll always remember this trip," she said.

"What did you think about Little Five?"

She laughed. "Oh, I've never seen anything like the beatniks," she said. "I've never known people that would just give up on living to do what they wanted. I couldn't imagine living without working."

He could see the joy in her eyes again.

"And I'll always remember looking into that little girl's eyes," she continued. "Never have I seen so much peace and happiness in a child's face."

They rode quietly.

"I never seen anything like that in my son's face," she said. "Every time I look into his eyes, all I see is pain and suffering and his need to be well."

She stopped.

He could see she was getting weepy again.

"Are you going to start crying again?"

"No," she said. "I'm finished. I'm ready to go home."

It was almost three p.m. that afternoon when Paul pulled the truck off the main highway on to the Duck Springs exit.

"I've got to hurry," she said. "The cow hasn't been milked."

"Where do you want me to drop you off?" Paul asked.

"Stop at the end of the bridge," she said. "I'll take the trail along the river and go in the back way."

Moments later, Paul turned the truck around and stopped at the designated spot. She reached for her suitcase.

"When will I see you again?"

"I don't know," she said. "You'll have to wait for a message."

He nodded his acceptance.

"I enjoyed my time with you," he said. "I love you."

"I love you too," she said. "Bye."

Without another word, she turned, opened the truck door, and got out. Then, he watched as, suitcase in hand, she walked unsteadily down the embankment to the river trail.

The following morning, Paul was at work early. Once he clocked in, Will called him aside.

"I saw you drop that little blonde off at the bridge yesterday afternoon," Will said. "Y'all have a good Thanksgiving?"

"Yeah, we were up to Atlanta."

Will started to tweak his mustache. Paul knew something very serious was coming next.

"You're playing a dangerous game," Will said. "You don't want her husband to find out what you're doing."

Paul studied him with answering

"Some men will kill you over things like that."

"I've escaped so far," Paul said.

Will didn't reply at first. "You're not the same person you were before we came to this job," Will said finally. "You've changed."

"Maybe a little," Paul replied. "Has it affected my work?"

"Oh no!" Will said. "Not at all; you're a still great worker."

"Then no harm, no foul."

Will inhaled and peered at him. "It's not really any of my business," Will said.

Paul nodded. "I'm going to start work," he said.

Will could see he wasn't getting through. "Go ahead," Will said.

Ghosts

Over the next few days, there were no messages. Every afternoon when he left work, Paul saw the big rig in the yard. As always, he watched her go about her daily chores, but there was no acknowledgement that he was in the world. One afternoon, as she started to the barn to milk, she did glance toward him and he waved, but she didn't respond. He wondered where he stood with her. The first three weeks of December passed.

On December 23, 1961, which fell on a Friday, Paul was preparing for Christmas. When he arrived at work that day, his plan called for him to work four hours, attend the company Christmas party that night, then leave the following morning to go to his father's home in Florida. As he maneuvered the motor grader along the north shoulder, he glanced intermittently toward the homestead. Just after nine, he saw the husband, Cassie, and Timmy leave in the old red pickup and head toward Duck Springs. Two hours later, they returned. Once parked, Cassie and her husband pulled a huge Christmas tree out of the truck bed and carried it into the house. Moments later, they returned and carried two armfuls of Christmas gifts into the house. Timmy followed them excitedly. Deep anger and jealousy filled Paul as he watched. *How had this happened,* he asked himself? How had he allowed himself to fall in love with a married woman? Why wasn't he there with her to decorate the tree, hang the lights, and wrap the gifts? He wondered why fate had seen fit for him to find the woman he loved and not be able to be with her at Christmas. Finally, just before noon, he returned the motor grader to the storage area and clocked out. He was glad the day was over.

As he started to his truck, Knox called to him. "What you doing for Christmas?"

"Going to spend it with my dad in Florida," he replied.

"Want some company?"

"Sure," Paul said. "What you got in mind?"

"Me and Pete wanted to get away for a few days," Knox said. "We'll take my truck and get a motel."

"No problem," Paul said. "My dad would love to meet you."

As Paul drove back to the motel, he was glad Knox and Pete were going with him. His father would enjoy the company and they would provide some help answering questions about the job. His father was always asking about his job. Also, they would provide small talk and help get his mind off Cassie.

At the company Christmas party that night, Paul drank himself into a stupor. He had to quell the raging sense of jealousy he had felt earlier that day. Long before the party ended, Paul passed out and Knox and Pete helped him back to his room and put him into bed. The next morning, Paul was up early and packed for the trip. Outside the motel, he met Knox and Pete and he instructed Knox to just follow him. It was five hours to his father's house in Ocala. As he cruised south, he knew he would be glad to see his father.

Late that afternoon, he arrived at his father's house. Upon their retirement in 1953, Paul's parents had sold the family farm in North Alabama and moved to the Florida home. After his wife died in 1956, Paul's father George, aged sixty-eight, had lived alone in the home. He spent his days reading, gardening, and puttering around with old cars. His social security benefits proved to be adequate for him to live on.

George was delighted to meet Knox and Pete. They spent the first night drinking beer, telling jokes, and talking about politics. Just before midnight, Knox and Pete returned to their motel.

* * * *

On the following day, Christmas Day, the four went to a local restaurant for the traditional Christmas meal of turkey, dressing, giblet gravy, vegetables, and cranberry sauce. After dinner, Knox announced that he and Pete were going into town to see a movie and would return in a few hours. Paul said that was fine. He didn't tell them he wanted to spend some time alone with his father.

Once Knox and Pete were gone, his father dozed off in a recliner. Bored, Paul wandered through the house. In his father's bedroom, he saw childhood photos of himself with his mother. There was one photo of him leaning on a pair of crutches. There were braces on his legs and his mother was standing beside him with her arm around him. His eyes filled with tears as he remembered his mother. She been the one who formed him as a man.

He remembered how the death of his mother had thrown his life into a tailspin. When his father called and told him his mother had passed, Paul was suddenly spiritually lost. He had been closer to his mother than he had ever been to another person on this earth. His father loved him, but his mother had been the one who was always there. His tender side, the sensitive side that loved poetry and enjoyed a beautiful sunset, he had inherited from his mother.

Paul had slept in his mother's bed until he was ten. His father kept saying he was too old to be sleeping with his mother at that age, but his mother said there was a special mother and son bond between them. When Paul was at physical therapy one day, he told the other boys that he still slept with his mother. They laughed. When he returned home and his mother came to his bed that night, he told her he wanted to sleep alone.

The days after his mother's funeral, Paul was inconsolable. When he was due to return to work, he told Will he needed some more time. Will agreed. For over a week, Paul tried to reconcile his feelings about the loss of his mother. Finally, after Paul failed to return to work, Will went looking for him. Will found him in bed in his motel room with the scattered remains of fast food and two empty whiskey bottles.

"You've got to come out of this," Will said. "You're going to drink yourself to death."

Paul didn't tell him he had a pistol inside the bedside table and was considering a solution even more drastic.

"Come on," Will said, pulling back the covers. "You've got to come out of this. You need to be around people. You need to get out and find yourself again."

Finally, Will managed to get him out of bed. After he was showered and shaved, Will sat with him at the motel restaurant and watched him eat a good meal.

"I want you at work tomorrow," he said. "No if, ands, or buts."

Paul knew Will was right. He had reached rock bottom.

"Can I count on you?" Will asked.

"I'll be there," Paul said.

The following morning, Paul, although still dealing with the grief of his mother's death, returned to work. By the end of the week, he had returned to his old self.

Two weeks later, Paul thanked Will. "You saved my life," he said. "I don't bear personal loss very well."

"I can see that," Will had replied.

* * * *

Ten minutes later, Paul wandered into the home's spare bedroom, the room his mother had prepared for him to sleep in when he was visiting. His old childhood toys and mementoes were scattered about the room. There was an old tricycle, a blue ribbon he had won in a 4-H contest, a school plaque for perfect attendance, a lamp he had made in high school woodshop, and an old baseball cap. For a moment, he lingered in front of the bookshelf. Immediately, his eyes fell on the collection of Poe's poems his mother had presented to him twenty-five years earlier. He took the book from the shelf. On the inside cover, he saw his mother's handwriting: "For my son Paul on his fifteenth birthday. I love you."

Paul flipped through the pages. The poem *Annabel Lee* was marked. He read his favorite lines.

For the moon never beams without bringing me dreams of the
beautiful Annabel Lee;
And the stars never rise, but I feel the bright eyes of the
beautiful Annabel Lee.

He loved those lines. He continued reading.

And neither the angels in heaven above,
Nor the demons down under the sea,
Can ever dissever my soul from the soul
Of the beautiful Annabel Lee.

He looked up from the book.

Instantly, his thoughts turned to Cassie. Like the narrator in the poem, he had met the great love of his life and they had "loved with a love that was more than love." Never could he imagine himself having a deeper love for a woman than he had for Cassie. Like the narrator, he couldn't keep his eternal love, but their hearts were so irretrievably entangled that nothing could ever tear them apart. He was sure of that. Their hearts and souls had been bound together for all time. In the years ahead, there would be other women, but there would only be one Cassie. She was his Annabel Lee. He had found her, but now, like the narrator in the poem, fate had destined that he lose her. He wondered how he would handle it.

Later that afternoon, Knox and Pete returned and announced they were leaving for Duck Springs. Paul said good-bye and thanked them for spending Christmas with him and his father. An hour after they were gone, Paul said good-bye to his father and started to his pickup truck. Once outside the house, he stopped. Somewhere in the distance, he could hear a choir singing "Away in a Manger." His mind wandered back to his boyhood days at the little country church in north Alabama he attended with his mother. He remembered Betty Jenkins always singing that song during Christmas celebrations. In his mind, he could hear Betty singing.

"Away in a manger, no crib for a bed, the little lord Jesus lay down his sweet head. The stars in the sky looked down where he lay, the little Lord Jesus asleep on the hay."

As he listened to the words, he could feel an agonizing loneliness creeping into the furthermost corners of his soul. The emptiness, the sense of loss, the loneliness was more than he could bear, he thought. He wanted to do something, anything to escape this terrible loneliness. *I can't live with this,* he thought. *I would rather die than live with this terrible loneliness.*

First Attempt

January 2, 1962 was a difficult day for Cassie. A New Year had arrived here and she was confronted with a dilemma unlike any she had ever known. Over and over in her mind, she searched for an answer, but she found none. She knew she had to make a decision.

In her journal that night, she wrote:

January 2, 1962: These are trying days for me. My poor heart is like a ragged shirt that has been torn one way, then another. While my life has been with Austin all these years, I have fallen in love with another man. A man who is totally different from my husband, a man who offers the romantic love and adventure I have longed for. Now I'm about to lose him and my heart will be dead again when he is gone...

She stopped writing and looked out the window.

I must make a decision. A decision that I have the will to live up to. I must tell Paul that my life has to go on without him. I must harden my heart and return to the life I knew before he and the highway project arrived. Although I have loved Paul like I have never loved a man, I must find the old Cassie. I must again find the person who was content to live day after day caring only for her husband and child. I have to do it for Timmy. Although I love this man so incredibly much,

I could never take Timmy away from his father. The poor child is already sick enough. God knows losing his father would kill him. No matter how much I love Paul, I could never leave Timmy. This torment inside my mind is slowly destroying me.

That night at dinner, her husband announced that he would be leaving the following morning to go to North Carolina. He would be gone for four days. The following morning, she left a message for Paul.

Tomorrow night 8:30. At the cane break.

The following night, after Timmy was asleep, she made her way through the broomsage patch to the cane break. Paul was waiting.

"You didn't bring anything?" he asked.

She shook her head in disgust. "No," she said. "I didn't bring anything. I didn't bring food. I didn't bring the quilt. I only brought myself. I came to say good-bye."

He peered silently at her.

"We can't go on," she said. "You know that."

Finally, he spoke. "I know! I know!" he said. "It's just killing me to leave you."

"It's hard for me too," she said. "But we have to do it."

She could see the anguish in his face.

"There is no way we can be together, is there?" he said finally.

She looked at him. "No!" she shouted. "This has to end. We can't have this both ways."

"You could get a divorce," he said.

She interrupted. "Stop! Stop!" she said. "Quit talking crazy. We've already talked about that. You're a free bird. Men like you never settle down."

"I could change," he said.

She laughed. "You're talking crazy," she said. "And you know it."

He inhaled resignedly.

"I guess you're right," he said.

"Then let's say good-bye," she said.

"I'm not sure I can live without you," he said.

"You've got to," she replied.

They were silent for a moment, then she burst into laughter.

"Why are you laughing?"

"On the way back from Atlanta," she said. "You were the one who was saying everything would be all right. You were the strong one."

He turned his back to her.

"You just can't get this through your head, can you?"

His back was still to her.

"Okay," she said finally. "I'm going to walk back up that trail and never see you again."

She turned and started walking away.

"Wait!" he said, turning and rushing to her. "At least let's say goodbye and leave one another happily."

She knew he was right. She peered into his eyes, then rushed into his arms.

"Look what we've done," she said, holding him tightly. "We've fallen in love and now we've got to tear ourselves apart."

Tears were streaming down her face as she held him with all her might. "Don't you understand," she shouted through her tears. "Now I've got to go away."

In frustration, she buried her face in his chest and sobbed uncontrollably.

"You don't have to go away," he said.

She pulled back from him and glared angrily at him.

"This is not one of your poems or some crazy daydream," she said. "This is the real world." For a brief moment, she peered at him, then started walking to the trail. "I'm leaving now," she said.

At the trailhead, she stopped and turned to look at him. Despite the reality of the situation, her heart reached for him with every fabric of her being.

For a long moment, they peered at one another.

"I love you so much," he said.

Suddenly, his longing was stronger than her will to resist.

"Oh God! I love you too," she said suddenly. Her eyes filled with tears.

He opened his arms.

She rushed to him. Their lips met and his hot kisses warmed the simmering fires within her. The old passions came bursting forth. He went for her bosom. She didn't resist.

"Come on," she said. "Let's go to the hay room."

Final Farewell

January 11, 1962 fell on a Friday. When the Gartman crew finished work that day, Will called a crew meeting at the storage facility.

"The Duck Springs project is finishing early," he began. "We had expected the job to last until late February, but due to good weather and few breakdowns, we're finishing almost five weeks early. The next job will be in Tennessee, and we will start moving the equipment next Tuesday. That's four days from today."

"Where's the new job in Tennessee?" Pete asked.

"Just outside Knoxville," Will said. "It's a big job. Three, maybe four years' work. I'll have the transport assignments on Monday morning. We'll start closing down and moving the equipment on Tuesday. You boys have a good weekend and I'll see you here Monday morning."

With the news, Paul knew he had to prepare for the worst. There was no getting around the fact that he would be leaving Georgia soon and probably never see Cassie again. He knew he would have to see her one more time. After work, he returned to the motel, showered and shaved, and had dinner at the restaurant. After darkness fell, he returned to the storage facility and scrambled down the embankment to the peach tree and left a note.

I am leaving with the crew on Tuesday morning to start a new job in Tennessee. Can you meet me Sunday afternoon at the cane break around 4 to say good-bye? If so, leave the calf in the front pasture on Saturday.

All weekend, he dreaded Sunday afternoon. He spent Friday and Saturday night with the crew drinking beer and playing pool, trying to not think about her, but it was hopeless. On Saturday morning, he drove to the storage facility. The calf was in the front pasture. She would be there to say good-bye.

Sunday afternoon turned off cold. Although the sun was bright, a cold north wind came whistling through the trees and brought the wind chill down to near twenty degrees. The previous night had left a dusting of snow and small patches remained in sunless areas as Paul made his way down the river trail. Along the edges of the river, the water slapped against thin encrustations of ice. The dogwoods, which had been alive and verdant during the summer, were now leafless and crusted with tiny icicles. As he walked, he wore a heavy coat, gloves, and a cap with furry earflaps. Once he arrived at the cane break, he could feel the desolation. The log where they had placed the quilt the previous summer to make love was encrusted with ice and tiny flakes of snow. He waited.

Across the river, at the wide point, he could see the migrating ducks. Thousands of ducks, pintails, brown ducks, mallards, and teals bobbed up and down in the windswept water. In places, the ducks were so thick they hid the water beneath them. In the distance, he could see more and more ducks coming in. Like giant bees, they were descending on the windswept water with a constant chorus of quacking and flapping wings. He waited.

Just after 4:15, he saw her coming through the broomsage patch. She was wearing a heavy sweater, long pants, and her head was tied up in a scarf. When she reached the end of the trail, she stopped and peered at him, then looked away. Each was afraid to meet the other's gaze. Finally, their eyes met and they rushed into one another's arms. Both had dreaded this moment.

For a long moment, neither spoke.

"I'm not sure I can do this," he said, wiping away the tears.

"You've got to do it," she said. "We have no choice."

She held his face in her hands and peered into his eyes.

"Let's be very calm and businesslike about this," she said.

He laughed. "My heart is breaking into millions of little pieces," he said.

"So is mine," she replied. "But we have to do it."

"I know you're right," he said.

"There is something I have to tell you," she said.

"What's that?"

"I'm pregnant with your child."

"Are you sure it's mine?"

She laughed out loud and shook her head in frustration. "Of course I'm sure," she said. "A woman knows."

"Oh great God," he said. "I want to see your belly."

Quickly, she unbuttoned the heavy coat and pulled up her shirt to reveal a noticeable bump.

"Oh great God," he said again, falling to his knees. For a long moment, as he kissed her belly, she held his head to her midsection.

Finally, his eyes brimming with tears, he stood up.

"What do you want me to do?" he asked.

"There is nothing you can do," she said, pulling down the shirt and re-buttoning the coat. "There's nothing either of us can do! This is our child. I intend to raise it and love it and be good to it."

Suddenly, her words registered.

"Oh, God!" he said, putting his hands to his head. He turned from her.

She stared helplessly at him.

"We agreed to be calm about this," she said.

"You're right," he said.

She went to him, took his face in her hands again, and peered into his eyes.

"You have to learn to live without me," she said. "Your life has to go on. So does mine."

He didn't look at her.

"I'll always have this," she said, holding her stomach. "I'll always have a part of you. In a way, we'll always be together."

"It won't be the same," he said.

"No, it won't be the same," she said, "but it's the best we can do in our situation."

"Where can I write you?" she asked.

"Just write to Gartman Construction, Nashville, Tennessee, in my name. I'll get it."

Her eyes were brimming with tears.

"Oh, Paul," she said. "Hold me for just a moment."

Again, he took her in his arms and held her tightly.

"I'm going to turn around and back walk up the trail," she whispered in his ear. "I'm not going to say good-bye. I'll never love another man like I love you. I know that and believe it with all my heart."

They were still holding one another tightly.

"Then we'll never see each other again?"

"Why do you have to say everything?" she said. "Just let it happen. I hate words."

"I'll always love you, Cassie," he said.

"I'll always love you too," she said.

He broke the embrace. "Now go!" he said. "Go! Go!"

Suddenly, their ears were filled with the explosive sound of flapping wings. At the sound, their eyes met for the last time.

Across the lake, thousands of ducks, which had been resting in the windswept water, were taking flight into the winter sky. In a hurried flurry of flapping wings and a deafening chorus of quacks, wave after wave of ducks took flight into the crimson dusk. As more and more ducks lifted off, thousands of others followed and, for a brief moment, the cloud of ducks blotted out the afternoon sun. Then, just as suddenly as it began, the ducks were gone and bright sunlight washed across the water again. Seconds later, Paul heard the sound of footsteps and a rustling in the broomsage. He didn't look back.

Quickly, he turned and started walking along the water's edge to his truck. As he walked, he had never felt such a terrible emptiness inside himself. It was as if the core of his being had been ripped away. Never had he known such deep feelings of darkness and despair. All he had to do now was learn to live with himself, he told himself. There had been many breakups with other women over the years. He had survived those. Why wouldn't he survive this one? he asked himself.

* * * *

January 8, 1962: I told Austin I was pregnant today. I told him I had conceived in early December the night he came in from the long trip to Kansas. At first, he was undecided at the thought of having an unplanned child, but the next morning, he said he was glad. He said he hoped the child didn't have the "family disease." He said at least another child would give little Timmy somebody to play with so he wouldn't have to be alone so much. He said he felt Timmy's condition would improve if he had a playmate. Someone to talk to and be friends with. He said he hoped the child was a boy. He said he didn't want me to strain myself while I was pregnant and I should do as little gardening and housework as I wanted. He said he wanted me to have a strong, healthy baby.

Letters/Notebook Entries

The new Tennessee project consisted of building nine miles of new two-lane highway—no bridges—which would connect suburban Knoxville to Lee's Junction, a small farming community to the east. When the Gartman crew arrived, state personnel had already completed surveys of the right-of-ways and much of the clearing had been done by state subcontractors. Gartman's job was to build the base and drainage for the center slab, finish the shoulders, and get the paving and striping done. Engineers estimated the project would take about three years.

Once the equipment was moved, the crew's newly adopted home was the Lookout Mountain Inn just outside Knoxville. It was a small but comfortable motel about four miles from the jobsite. It had an adequate restaurant and bar and a gym for exercising. Also, there was a nursing school nearby and Will joked to the crew that it would provide a constant parade of women for the single crewmembers.

Over the first few months, Paul did everything in his power to keep Cassie out of his mind. First, he threw himself headlong into his work. Day after day, he arrived at work early and put in as much overtime as possible. Also, he promised himself he was going to learn to read blueprints. For years, he had watched Will and the superintendent pore over blueprints, discussing this or that detail of some project. Often, he would gather around a blueprint with the other crewmembers as Will explained some fine point of construction. Paul would look at the blueprint and pretend to understand, but really, it was just a gibberish of blue markings, coded lines, and meaningless numbers. Two days after he was settled in to the new job, Paul borrowed some old blueprints from Will and promised to study them. He needed something to help him keep his mind off Cassie.

Over the first few months, he lived with an agonizing loneliness he could never have imagined. *It was so ironic*, he thought. He had had all sorts of women available to him over the years. In fact, he had spent lots of time pushing them away. Now that he had found the woman of his dreams, fate had destined that he could not have her for his own. She belonged to another man.

Something was happening to him. He wasn't sure what it was. He didn't have Cassie, yet his love for her drove him away from other women. After he left Duck Springs, his emotions slowly began to freeze up inside him. He wasn't sure how it was happening, but he could feel his feelings being somehow caged inside himself. Many days, he thought about the child she was carrying. He had always wanted a child, but now he would never have an opportunity to be a father to the child. All of his dreams had come true, then been dashed.

For almost five months, there was no communication between them and he seemed to be winning the battle. During the days, work provided a distraction from his deep longing, but at night, he was helpless. Most nights were spent with the crew at the motel bar drinking, shooting pool, and chatting. There, he would drink himself into a stupor. Some nights, the loneliness would be so great the beer would not suffice and he would turn to hard whiskey. This would numb his brain, but the following morning with the hangovers, he felt like dying.

Some nights, Paul would go to Will's home for a home-cooked meal. Will's wife Margie loved to make over Paul. She had grown up in Birmingham and loved to talk to a fellow Alabamian. Other nights, he would go see a movie with Knox or Pete. He was trying to keep his deep-seated feelings for Cassie under wraps in the back of his mind. It was like putting a mask on a pretty face. The reality could be smothered for a while, but the truth of his love always managed to rear its ugly head. It worked for a while. Then, in mid-May, all that changed.

One afternoon, after finishing work, Paul parked his machine in the company storage area and clocked out. As he started for his truck, he heard Will call. He turned and saw his foreman coming toward him. He was carrying something.

"The main office sent me a letter addressed to you with this week's payroll," Will said.

Paul peered curiously at him, then took the letter. The return address was Audrey Ponder, P.O. Box 523, Duck Springs, GA.

"Thanks!" Paul said.

In his truck, he slid under the steering wheel and slammed the door, then he opened the letter.

May 22, 1962

Dear Paul:

This is Cassie. I am using my sister's name and post office box address to write you.

I hope you are well and enjoying your new job in Tennessee. I've never been to Tennessee, but I've heard it's a beautiful state. My sister worked for a while in a tourist resort in Gatlinburg and she said the trees and mountains were so beautiful in the fall of the year.

I just wanted to let you know I still love you and think about you every day. I'm big as a barrel with your child. I've had a few problems with morning sickness, but not like I had with Timmy. The doctor said less morning sickness means a healthier baby. If I get cold or hungry, he kicks like a mule inside me. He's going to be as big and strong and smart as his father. I hope he has the same gentleness. I don't want a hard, cold son that is afraid to show his emotions because he feels it is unmanly. I have known too many men like that in my life. The doctor said I should deliver in mid-August.

Oh, Paul, I miss you so. At times, this loneliness is unbearable. I need to laugh. I need someone to talk to. I need someone to show me something different. The torment I have been feeling lately has reached the point that I can't eat, although I know I should. I have this child inside me and it needs nourishment.

Today, when I was milking the cow, I wished so much that you would suddenly appear in the barn hallway and take me into your arms. I long for you to take away from this terrible loneliness. I need you to steady my mind.

You can write me at the above name and address. That's my sister Audrey's old post office box she used before she moved away. It's paid up for five years, so I can use it a long time. The only person who has a key is me, so it will be safe to send me letters. Any letters I send you will be from her.

What are you doing every day? Tell me about your new life. I'd love to hear about it. Please send me photos of you at your new job.

Please stay well.

Love,

Cassie

He looked up from the letter. Suddenly, all of the old feelings he had kept at bay over the past five months came sweeping back over him. Now, as he considered the fact that she was having his son, he was being pulled ever closer to her.

Inside himself, more than ever, he felt this deep longing to be near her, to touch her, to see her smile, to hear her voice, and to smell her breasts. Whether he wanted to admit it or not, she was like a drug from which he was unable to wean himself. Part of him wished she had never written.

That night, he dreamed he was in bed with Cassie in her pregnancy. As always, they laughed and kissed and joked and talked about anything and everything. In the dream, he held his hand to her belly and felt the child kick. He promised to help her change the diapers and get up in the middle of the night to give the baby its bottle. He told her he wanted to be a good father and help her raise the child to be a good, honest, intelligent person. He wanted the three of them to be a happy family together.

Suddenly, he woke up. He looked at the clock. It was 3:30. He had to work the next day. Restless and tormented, he got out of bed. For almost an hour, he was unable to sleep. He had half a bottle of bourbon in his bedside table. He drank it straight and chased it with tap water. Finally, he went back to bed and managed to sleep for about an hour before he had to get up for work.

Over the next few days, he considered writing back. He knew that once he sat down to write, the old feelings of closeness and intimacy would take center stage again. He was afraid of that. On the other hand, he knew he should write back to honor the commitment they had made to one another when they said good-bye. At least he should do that. The love in his heart wanted her to know he was okay. On Friday of the following week, he decided to reply.

May 30, 1962
Paul Hamilton
C/O Gartman Highway Construction
Nashville, Tennessee

Dear Cassie:

Thanks so much for your letter.

The Tennessee job is going well. Day after day, I do basically the same thing that I did in Georgia. Tennessee is colder than Georgia, but the countryside is beautiful.

Nothing would please me more than to be with you in your pregnancy, but I know that's an impossibility. I can only stand back and watch and hope that you and the baby will be well.

Over the past year, we have really gotten ourselves into a pickle. Here we are deeply in love and about to have a child, yet you are married and I'm more than 600 miles away. It's crazy what we have done. It's crazy how we have let ourselves go with one another without any thought of the consequences. It is so wild that I have found the woman I love with all my heart and I can't have her with me every day. I guess, like the old saying, you can't choose who you fall in love with.

Oh, my sweet darling Cassie, I miss you so. Just to be near you to hold you and touch you would mean everything in the world to me. Like you, I remember our happy times together. Our time at the cane break and in Atlanta are some of the happiest memories of my life.

Although we are many miles apart, you live in my heart every minute of every day. I could never love another woman the way I love you. What the results of that will be, I don't know. I do know I will always love you.

I will close for now. I am so sad.

Write me when the baby is born and send photos.

Love,
Paul

Two days later, Knox, who had one of the new Polaroid instant cameras, made photos of Paul on a motor grader and a compactor with the Tennessee countryside in the background. That afternoon, Paul slipped the photos inside the letter and mailed it.

* * * *

Over the next few months, Paul returned to his normal routine of working during the days and spending nights with the crew. As always, Cassie was on his mind. The hot summer months of July and August passed and the cool days of early September came around. He received another letter.

September 4, 1962
Dear Paul:
I hope you're happy and healthy and your job is going well.
On August 17, I gave birth to Paul Austin Carter, an eight-pound, three-ounce baby boy. I told Austin I wanted to name him Paul because that was my father's name. Austin agreed and said we would call him Paulie. He is a healthy baby with brown eyes and dark, curly hair like his father. Already, in his eyes, I can see you. Sometimes, when he's nursing, he looks up at me and I am so reminded you.
Outside of the birth of Paulie, nothing else has changed much in my life. Last week, for no reason, Timmy started having seizures. It almost scared me to death. I called the ambulance and they took him to the hospital. He was there for three days, then he came back home. The doctors raised the dosage levels on his medicine. He seems to be fine now.
As I write that, I am wishing you were here tonight. As always, I am so alone. My mind knows you're gone, but my heart yearns to be with you. How I long to be near you and

feel your strength. You always had a way of making me feel truly loved. That's what I miss the most.

With this pregnancy, I didn't have much of a garden this year. We had plenty of tomatoes and some squash, but I didn't plant pole beans because I couldn't get down on my hands and knees to string them. There wasn't much rain this year and the sweet corn didn't do worth a flitter. I planted four rows. They came up, got about four feet high, and tasseled way too early. I fed the stunted little ears to the cow. I did manage to pick most of the peaches and get them in a can. I got 38 quarts.

I keep on running on with this letter because, when I'm writing you, I feel close to you. You live in my heart every day and I hope that maybe someday, we'll see each other again. I don't know when, but at least I can hope.

I'll close for now.

Hope you like the photos of the baby.

Love,
Cassie

Included in the letter were four photos of a three-week-old baby. His eyes filled with tears as he gazed at the photos. They reminded him of old baby photos of himself.

That afternoon, after Paul clocked out, Will said he and the other crewmembers would meet in the restaurant later.

"I think I'll stay in tonight," Paul said. "I want to study the blueprints and get a good night's sleep."

"Suit yourself," Will said.

Back at the motel room, he showered and took a nap. He dreamed that he and Cassie and the baby were together. He dreamed Cassie was sitting in a chair in his motel room, nursing the child. As he gazed at her, he felt the sight was the most beautiful thing he had ever seen. The woman he loved with all his heart was nursing their child. He was moved to tears at the sight.

Suddenly, he awoke. He turned on the light and looked at the clock. It was 7:30 at night. In his mind, he wanted to die. He couldn't sleep anymore; there was too much torment in his mind. Finally, he got up and went to the motel restaurant. Once he sat down, he realized he didn't want to eat. All he wanted to do was drink. He politely excused himself when the waitress arrived, and went to the bar. After a few beers, they weren't getting the job done and he turned to whiskey. Finally, he passed out and fell on the floor. The bartender knew Paul was part of the Gartman crew and he contacted the front desk, who roused Will out of bed. Together, Will and Knox carried Paul out of the bar and helped him into bed.

* * * *

Over the next few months, Paul's emotions continued to freeze up. His feelings that were once like a great waterfall that in the warmth of summer had flowed wildly and freely, now, during the cold months of winter, had frozen into a hard mass of solid, unyielding ice. His only protection from this slow glaciation was his job. It was a distraction, the only survival technique he had to put Cassie and the baby out of his mind. If he allowed himself to be too near his emotions, he was afraid he would start to lose it.

The rest of that summer, there was no further communication. With each passing day, part of him longed to receive another letter. On the other hand, he feared what effect it would have on him. Finally, the alcohol was all that could save him. There were other women he met in the motel bar, but he had no interest in them. It was Cassie he wanted in his arms at night.

September and October gave away to winter. In late November, an early snow swept across northern Tennessee and the crew lost more than a week's work. Finally, the harsh cold of late December arrived.

* * * *

On Dec. 21, 1962, after the company Christmas party, Paul prepared for his annual trek to south Florida. After he was six hours south of Knoxville, he decided to spend the night in Atlanta. At first, he thought he would spend the night at the Jefferson Davis Inn, but he was afraid it would bring back too many memories. Although he was tired, he continued driving for two more hours and finally stopped in Macon for the night. Early the next morning, he was up and on the road again.

When he pulled off the main highway onto the Duck Springs exit, it was early morning. As he approached, he glanced at the homestead. The big rig was in the yard, but there was no activity. He drove past the homestead, then turned around in the old company storage area and parked on the west end of the bridge. It was 7:30. On the clothesline, he could see a string of white diapers intermixed with several dresses and overalls. The vegetable garden lay fallow. The calf he had saved her from was much larger now and grazing in the back pasture. The peach trees had grown. In the house, he knew they were preparing for Christmas. He wondered what his son was doing. Finally, having seen enough, he fired up the truck and pulled back out on the highway.

* * * *

For 1963, Paul had renewed his resolution to master blueprints. Over the past year, with constant study and questions for Will, he had become quite knowledgeable about the various codes and markings. At one point, he had spoken to Will about taking a drafting class at a local technical school, but Will said that would be more trouble than it was worth. Such a school teaches people to draw, not to read blueprints, Will said. He told Paul that if he had questions, he could come to him with them. Paul agreed.

Throughout the months of January and February, Paul was on a compactor. The project was nine miles long and had been divided up into three-mile segments. This meant he would make a three-mile run from one end of a segment to another. Unlike the Duck Springs job when he would be on an earthmover one day and a motor grader the next, here he could be on the same machine for two weeks at a time.

One afternoon in mid-March, Paul was on a compactor bringing the base up to soil compaction standards. While the first segment of the project was surrounded by flat land, the second segment was surrounded by mountains. Day after day, Paul would run the compactor the full three-mile length of the second segment, watching as the landscape along either side of the roadway changed from low-lying buttes to high, craggy mountains. Near the start of the middle segment, Knox was on a bulldozer some thirty to forty yards up the side of the mountain. Paul knew working on the steep incline with the dozer was dangerous. At one point, he stopped to talk to Knox.

"Knox," Paul said. "Be careful taking that dozer up the side of that mountain with all the loose rocks and shale..."

"Why?" Knox said.

"If that dozer starts sliding in those loose shale and rocks," Paul said, "you and that machine could come tumbling down the side of that mountain."

"Naw," Knox said confidently. "If it started sliding, I'd jump off."

Paul shook his head. "I'd be careful," he said.

That afternoon. Paul was back on the compactor, passing up and down the middle segment. Intermittently, he watched as Knox took the bulldozer up the sharp mountain grade again and again. At one point, the dozer started to slide and Knox moved one track slightly sideways and stopped the sliding. During the next pass, in deeper shale this time, the dozer started sliding again, but when Knox pulled the track to the side again, the shale and loose rocks gave way and the dozer kept sliding. Paul watched in horror as the bulldozer came sliding down the mountainside, gathering speed. As it slid, the right track hit a huge boulder and the dozer flipped and began to tumble sideways down the mountainside.

"Jump! Jump!" Paul shouted.

Knox jumped, but it was too late.

As he jumped, the already tumbling bulldozer struck his body and knocked him directly into its path.

Paul watched in horror as the bulldozer rolled over Knox's body and finally stopped on the road shoulder, its engine still running.

"Holy Christ," Paul said.

Up the road, he could see Pete on a motor grader and he started waving his arms frantically. Moments later, Pete appeared and Paul pointed towards Knox's body and the overturned dozer.

"Oh my God!" Pete said.

"Go get Will," Paul ordered. "Tell him to call an ambulance. I'll see what I can do for Knox."

Instantly, Pete, running the motor grader at full speed, raced off to find Will.

Moments later, Paul stopped the compactor in front of Knox's body. The moment he got off the machine and started running to Knox, he knew it was going to be bad. As he knelt over his old friend, he could see Knox was dying.

"Knox! Knox!" Paul said.

Blood was coming out of Knox's nose and mouth, and he was gasping for breath. Paul could see his chest had been crushed and he knew he was dying from internal bleeding.

"Knox! Knox!" Paul called. "Hold on! Hold on! We're going to get an ambulance."

Knox, his eyes wide open, smiled faintly.

"Ambulance ain't going to do me no good," he said.

For a moment, Knox stared straight into Paul's eyes, then raised his hand. Paul took his friend's hand and held it for a brief moment. Then Knox's hand went limp and, for a long moment, he peered into Paul's eyes. Knox smiled faintly, then his body went limp.

Paul, tears filling his eyes, shook his head in anguish.

Two days later, the company shut down the job for a day so crewmembers could go to Huntsville, Alabama to bury Knox. As Paul, Will, Charley, Pete, and Knox's family members carried the casket across the cemetery grounds, Paul wondered about his own death. Would it occur on a construction machine like Knox? Would he die of old age? Would it have anything to do with his love for Cassie?

The hot days of June and July passed. In early August, Paul knew he would be getting a letter from Cassie soon. Little Paulie would be one in mid-August. A week later, Will handed him a letter.

August 23, 1963

Dear Paul:

I hope you are happy and healthy and your job is going well.

Last week, Paulie celebrated his first birthday. He is such a happy baby. Lately, he's been irritable because he is teething, but most of the time, he is interested in anything and everything. He has nine baby teeth and I plan to stop nursing and take start feeding him solid food soon.

I had a good garden this year. The Farmers' Almanac *predicted lots of rain in May and June and that's exactly what happened. You wouldn't believe how much sweet corn, tomatoes, and okra I canned this year. I gave a lot of the okra and tomatoes to Mrs. Simpson, my neighbor down the road. To be honest, I just got sick and tired of canning. As for peaches, I got 58 quarts. That's a lot of peach cobblers.*

Austin said he was getting a raise at the end of the year and was going to buy a deep freezer for Christmas. Hallelujah! No more standing over the hot stove in July and August and watching steam blow out of that pressure cooker. I'll be so happy.

Last night, I dreamed you were in my bed, making love to me. Although you are far away, I think of you and need you so. I want to yield to his strength and have you save me from this loneliness. Are you thinking of me? I hope so. I miss you so.

As always, you are on my mind.

Hope you like the new baby pictures.

Love,
Cassie

Included were three photos of a year-old child with a shock of dark hair, brown eyes, and dressed in bib overalls. Paul smiled with pure joy as he gazed at the photos. Again, he was reminded of photos of himself as a baby.

A week later, he penned a reply. Although he missed her with every fabric of his being, he didn't want to pour out the depths of his feelings for her. It was as if he was dredging up a part of his past that had been dredged over long enough. He tried to keep it short.

September 2, 1963

Dear Cassie,

My heart soars with gladness when I see photos of our son. I only wish I could be there with you and him, but I know that is not possible.

I'm happy to hear you are doing well and had a good garden this year.

Take care, stay well, and please take care of our son. He's such a beautiful child. I couldn't be prouder.

You're in my thoughts every minute of every day.

Love,
Paul

* * * *

When Cassie read his reply, she somehow sensed, for the first time, a lingering divide between them. She wasn't sure why. The following day, she made a new entry in her journal.

Nov. 28, 1963. I dreamed about Paul last night. I dreamed we were at the cane break on the old quilt, loving one another over and over with all our might. We were like two wild animals clawing at the very heart and soul of one another. Anybody who would had seen us would have had a hard time figuring out if we were fighting or making love. It was always that way with Paul. So intense and so satisfying! I guess I was lucky to have known a man like him. He was one of a kind!! But it was just a dream. Nothing more than me wishing for things that can never be again. Paul is gone. I know that. Paul is gone. I know that. I must keep telling myself that so it will seep into my hard head.

* * * *

At the 1963 Gartman Christmas party, Will announced the company was giving Paul a new Ford truck. Usually, the company would give senior crewmembers a new truck every five years. Although Paul had had the old truck almost six years, Will had been promising a new one for the past two. The morning after the party, Will and Paul drove to the dealership in Knoxville. Once he was handed the keys, he moved all of his personal belongings, including his .38 special, to the new truck. Then he said good-bye to Will and was en route to his father's house in Florida for Christmas.

Nine hours later, Paul was in south Georgia. It was around noon when he arrived at the homestead. The day had turned off bright and sunny and was an unseasonably warm day for late December. As always, he drove past the homestead, turned around, and parked on the west end of the bridge. The moment he parked the truck, his heart leapt with joy. There in the grass in the backyard, he saw Cassie playing with Paulie. The child was dressed in blue baby overalls and a white shirt and, at age one, he was just learning to walk. Cassie would stand behind him holding his hands, then set him free and he would take five or six uncertain steps then sit down. Cassie would stand him up again, then the child would take another seven or eight steps and sit down again. Moments later, the child was on its feet again, and Cassie chased it playfully as the child, giggling with delight, tried to escape. Finally, she caught up to the child and swept it up in her arms as it laughed happily. His eyes filled with tears. Oh, how he wished he could be there. Just to hold the baby and look into his eyes. Just to kiss the child and tell him he loved him. He watched the mother and child playing for almost an hour, knowing all the while, that, no matter how much he loved them, he could never be with them. Finally, the mother swept the child up into her arms and went back inside. Ten minutes later, as he drove south on the main highway, he wanted to die.

Torment

In early January of 1964, Cassie's life was fuller than ever. With another child in the house, there was never enough time. There were more meals to be cooked, more dishes to be washed, milk to be churned, diapers to be washed, and the house to clean. Timmy had to have his medicine, Paulie needed a new pacifier, and bills had to be paid. There was simply not enough time in the day. Even further, she was desperately struggling with her personal thoughts and her promise to Paul. As always, her favorite time of the day was her quiet time when she could sit down with her notebook and pour out her thoughts.

January 13, 1964: I must make a decision. A decision that I have the will to live up to. I must find the strength to go on living without Paul. Although I made a sacred promise to him, my life must continue. I must harden my heart and return to the life I knew before he and the highway project arrived. Although I will love Paul like I have never loved a man, I must find the old Cassie. I must again find the person who was content living day after day taking care of her husband, her home, and her children. Somehow, I must find the strength to make this decision.

February 4, 1964: It's raining outside tonight. In the west, I hear loud booms of thunder and big sheets of wind and rain slapping again the windows and the sides of the house. I cannot describe the loneliness I am feeling. My poor heart is like a fallow garden that has no one to till the soil, trim away the weeds, or add fertilizer and water to make it come alive. Paul has been gone over two years. The man I loved so much will never touch me again. I'm sure of that. I hate it, but in my mind, I can feel him fading away. He will always live in my heart, but my life has to go on. I know I must say good-bye.

She looked up from the writing. Her eyes began to fill with tears. For several minutes, she broke down in uncontrollable sobs. Huge tears ran down her cheeks and fell on the bed cover and the sleeve of her nightgown. Finally, she regained herself and continued writing.

Day after day, my life is like a movie I have seen a hundred times. It's the same thing over and over. Every morning, I get up and watch the sunrise. I keep the house clean, wash the clothes, take care of Timmy and Paulie, milk the cow, churn the butter, cook the meals, and watch the sun set. Next month, I'll start a new garden again. When it comes in, I'll pick and pare and pack and can food for another year. It's like I'm stuck in a train station with trains passing on either side and I have nowhere to go. Tonight, as I lie here alone in my bed, I feel my body aching for the touch of a man, yet I have nowhere to release it. My life has to go on without Paul.

* * * *

During the first few months of 1964, the Knoxville project was moving into its third segment. During most of March, Paul was on an earthmover, dredging up ton after ton of topsoil for the third segment's center base. The company had hired a new man to replace Knox. Bobby was a quiet, forever smiling young man in his late twenties. He loved to play checkers and, many nights, Paul and Bobby played checkers in Bobby's room while the other crewmembers drank in the bar. Some nights, Paul would go to Will's house for a home-cooked meal. Most nights, he would have questions about blueprints. Although Paul tried to stay busy, not a day passed that Cassie wasn't on his mind.

Then, in late August, he received a new letter.

August 28, 1964

Dear Paul:

I hope you're happy and healthy and your job is going well.

Paulie turned two last week. The older he gets, the more he looks and acts like you. Last Christmas, I bought him a toy bulldozer and he loves to play with it in the yard. Just yesterday, we were in the toy store in Albany and he cried until I bought him one of those grading machines with the blade on the bottom. Remind you of anyone you know?

He's eating solid food now. Sometimes, I catch him playing with his food and he will get that faraway look in his eyes just like his daddy. He's got thirteen baby teeth. I've started toilet training him. You won't believe how sick and tired I am of washing diapers.

Just wanted to drop you a line. I walked down behind the barn today and I was thinking about you. The path from the spring to the cane break is all grown over now. It's like you and I had never been there. I wanted to tell you I love little Paulie with all my heart. As long as I have him, I'll have a part of you.

I hope you stay happy and healthy and moving on with your life.

Sincerely,
Cassie

As he looked up from the letter, he wondered why she didn't end it with "Love, Cassie." Why had she had used the word "sincerely?"

During the days ahead, he struggled to maintain his peace of mind. With all his being, he tried to keep Cassie out of his mind, but the only real solution was alcohol. Night after night, he would join the other crewmembers to drink. He would start with a couple beers, then graduate to hard whiskey. His favorite drink was screwdrivers, a combination of orange juice and vodka. He knew it was the only real solution he had that would free up his mind from the memories and the hopeless love he had for Cassie.

Over the past year, he could sense something was happening to his mind, but he wasn't sure what. He had always been a person who was very self-aware. He had read Freud and Jung and he recalled Socrates' words that the greatest knowledge a man could have was self-knowledge. Despite this, something was happening to his mind, his thought processes, his perceptions, but he couldn't identify it.

Sometimes, on the job, his thoughts would become fragmented. His vision would get blurry. At times, he seemed to have no control over his senses. Things would appear then disappear, then reappear again. He would sense something moving out of the corner of his eye, then he would look to identify it and nothing was there. At other times, he would see shadows, then look again and there were none. Once, when he was driving in the night, he thought he saw Cassie holding a baby on the side of the road, waving to him. Then when he got closer, he saw it was just a mailbox.

Over the next few months, he started having a recurring dream. In the dream, he was a little child lost in deep woods at night and surrounded by wild animals. Suddenly, he would wake up and be trembling with fright. He knew he had to pull himself together, but he wasn't sure how to do it. He couldn't tell anyone. They would say he was losing his mind. For the first time in his life, he was afraid. He had to find his old self and regain his peace of mind and his senses.

During August and September, he spent more and more time alone. He told himself he was weary of being around the other crewmembers. He had heard all their stories, he knew their likes and dislikes and their beliefs about religion, politics, and women. So, instead of drinking with the crew, he would buy a fifth of vodka and a quart of orange juice and going back to his room to drink alone. He found that he especially liked to drink alone during a rain.

* * * *

His behavior didn't go unnoticed. During the last week in September, Will pulled him aside.

"What's going on with you?" he asked. "You don't like to drink with me and the boys anymore?"

"Sometimes, I just want to be alone."

"You've been doing a lot of that lately," Will said. "Are you sure you're okay?"

"I'm fine," Paul said. "I'm just trying to figure out some things in my head."

Will peered at him. "I'm worried about you," he said. "You haven't been the same since we finished the Duck Springs job."

"What are you talking about?"

"That blonde put some kind of spell on you," Will continued. "I'm not sure what, but you're a totally different person."

Paul didn't answer at first. "That may be part of it," he said finally. "But I'll get over it. Just give me some time."

Will peered at him thoughtfully. "You know the company medical plan will pay for you to see a psychologist," he said.

Paul laughed. "A psychologist? What the hell would I do with a psychologist?"

"Those guys can talk to you and help you understand your personal problems."

"Nobody could ever know my mind better than me."

"If you want to deny it, go ahead," Will said. "But I'm telling you there's something bad wrong going on with you."

Paul had heard enough. "I'm going to start work," he said.

Will could see he was wasting his breath. "Go on," he said. "You never listen to me anyway..."

* * * *

The summer of 1964 had been a busy one for Cassie. As always, during July and August, she was busy storing food, but this year, it was a cakewalk. She had a new freezer and the time she had spent storing food had been cut by more than half. With the freezer, once the food was picked and prepared, all she had to do was stuff it into a freezer bag and stack it in the freezer. No more standing over a hot stove with a steaming pressure cooker. No more packing fruit jars and tightening the lids. The deep freezer had given her a new lease on life. Also, Timmy seemed to be doing better. Austin had been right about one thing. Now that Paulie was in the house, Timmy was a happier, much more outgoing child. He loved to spend endless hours watching Paulie play. Timmy was there to cater to Paulie's every need and wanted to help his mother by changing Paulie's diapers and giving him his bottle.

August 30, 1964: DeWayne Glover is such a nice man. Today, he came to collect for Austin's life insurance, but I didn't have the money. I told him my husband had been gone for almost two weeks and I wouldn't have the money until he returned. I asked if he could wait until next month to get the money. He said that would be fine. When he looks me, I can see the hunger in his eyes. I know he is attracted to the woman in me.

September 12, 1964: It is raining again tonight. It is one of the misting rains that comes before the cold of the holidays. Austin has been on the road for over two weeks and I am lonely and frightened again. When the night comes, I yearn for the touch of a man's hands on my body. Oh, how I would love to fold myself into the arms of a loving man and, ever so quietly and gently, release this terrible longing in my loins. Paul has been gone for over two years. As much as I love him, I can't wait forever for him. My life has to go on.

September 21, 1964: Every fall, this same old loneliness comes back to me. As the days grow shorter and the holidays get closer, my spirit reaches out for someone to touch, to feel, to hold. With the cold weather and the holidays coming, people need other people. Holidays are a time for being together, not apart. Austin has been gone for almost two weeks. He has made one trip to California and back. Now he is somewhere in Missouri, going to Oregon. He promised he would be home for Christmas and the kids. Paul is no longer a part of my life. As always, I'm alone.

September 30, 1964: Today, DeWayne came back to the house to get the check for Austin's life insurance. Timmy was at school. When I handed him the check, he said it must be lonely out here at the homestead with my husband gone all the time. He told me again I was an attractive woman and I shouldn't have to live like this. I told him I was married. He said that was okay. He was too. Down deep inside, I wanted to tell him I would like to meet him, but I was afraid. I made a promise to Paul, but this constant need for a man is making me crazy. Oh, how I long for the touch of a man! How I would love to release this terrible burden inside me! Although I made a promise to Paul, I do have the right to change my mind. I'm a woman. If DeWayne makes the offer again, I'm going to accept.

Oct. 10, 1964: Today I was back at Glover's General Store and DeWayne helped me out to the truck with my groceries. After he closed the truck door, he said he would love to talk privately with me and share his life. He said, like me, he was married with children but he was always alone. He said he had a wife, but, after seven years of marriage and two children, they had become like brother and sister. As I listened, I knew this store of passion inside me was greater than my will to say no. Before I drove away, I told DeWayne I would leave him a message in the fruit jar at the far peach tree. He smiled and said good-bye.

* * * *

During the last week in November, Paul was on a motor grader cutting shoulder base to grade. Day after day, he would move slowly along the tightly compacted shoulders and shave off just enough fill dirt to match the markings on the grade stakes. Once grading was complete, several inches of drainage gravel would be placed atop the base, then topsoil would be added for the grassing crew.

On Thursday of that week, Paul had spent all morning making the shoulder cuts. Early that afternoon, Will stopped to inspect his work. After parking his truck, Will walked along the shoulder base checking the cuts against the stake markings. Suddenly, he turned.

"Paul!" he shouted.

Paul turned at the sound of the foreman's voice.

Will was glaring angrily at him. He motioned for Paul to shut down the motor grader and come to him. Moments later, Paul was at his side.

"What the hell is going on with you?" he shouted, pointing to the shoulder cuts. "Look at this!! You cut this base down eight inches. We only needed three. Didn't you look at the stakes?"

Will had never talked to him like that.

Paul looked at the markings on the stakes, then at the cuts. Will was right; he had made the cuts five inches lower than the grade markings. For a moment, Paul was shocked. The mistake was plain as day. What was he thinking?

Paul shrugged. "Sorry," he said. "I guess I just wasn't paying attention."

"Wasn't paying attention?" Will said angrily. "What kind of excuse is that? This is going to cost us a full day's work. Now we're got to fill in again, pack it down, and cut it again. That's several thousand dollars!"

For a moment, Will stopped himself and turned his back to Paul to hide his anger. Finally, he turned to face him. "If the old man finds out, he'll tell me to fire you," Will said, calmer now.

Paul inhaled resignedly. "I don't know what to say," Paul said. "It's a mistake. I made it. What else can I say?"

Will shook his head helplessly. "I want you to take a few days off," he said finally.

"I don't want to take any time off," Paul replied. "It was a simple mistake."

"Don't argue with me," Will said. "This is several thousand dollars you cost the company. Take the rest of today off and go somewhere for a few days. Just try to get yourself together."

Paul knew it was useless to argue.

"Go on!" Will said. "Clock out and be back here Monday morning."

Paul dejectedly turned away.

* * * *

When he arrived back at the motel room, his thoughts were in shambles. It was if his mind couldn't take any further strain. It was one thing to deal with the torment of missing Cassie, but it would be even worse to lose his job. Back at the motel, he packed a suitcase and went to his truck. When he started the engine, he didn't know where he was going. He was going anywhere. He was going to do anything to relieve the agonizing torment in his mind. He decided he would drive south for two hours, then wherever he was, he would stop and get a motel room.

* * * *

Two hours later, he was in Gatlinburg. As he approached the downtown area, he was taken aback by the autumn colors of the Smoky Mountains. After renting a motel room, he decided he was going to make the best of the next two days. He was going to relax, read a book, go for a hike in the mountains, and try to get his mind off Cassie. Also, he vowed to not drink. Drinking was part of the problem, he told himself. That night, after dinner, he watched *Wagon Train* on the television for a while, then went to bed.

After breakfast the following morning, he went to a local bookstore and purchased a book about Nazi Germany. Back at the motel, he packed lunch and the book into a backpack and went for a hike in the mountains. The hiking path through the mountains was a five-mile circular trail. From the first step, the entire journey was a breathtaking visual feast. Up and down he went along the mountain trail. Everywhere, the trees—oaks, maples, sweet gums and poplars—were ablaze with color. Deep scarlet reds, blazing yellows, rich browns, and savage greens adorned the trail on either side. He was so happy to walk among such natural beauty. As he strode along the trail, he wished with all his heart that Cassie and the baby were with him. Nothing would please him more than sharing this natural beauty with the people he loved most.

Back at the motel that afternoon, he was tired from the five-mile hike, but he had enjoyed himself. After a nap, he read the book on Nazi Germany, then went to dinner for a meal of southern fried chicken, mashed potatoes and gravy, green beans, steam rolls, and iced tea with extra lemon. That night, back in the motel room, he finished the book around ten p.m. and went to bed.

When he awoke Sunday morning, he felt good. Will was right. He needed some time off to pull himself together and find his center of gravity again. He told himself he should listen to Will more often. That morning, he read the local newspaper, browsed through another bookstore, then around 11:30, went to lunch.

When he emerged from the restaurant and started down the sidewalk to his truck, he glanced across the street. As he did, he saw a smallish woman, late twenties with her blonde hair in a ponytail, striding down the sidewalk holding the hand of a dark-haired toddler. He stopped and peered at the woman and child. It looked like Cassie and Paulie. Paul did a double take.

What was Cassie doing in Tennessee? *It can't be*, he thought. He was sure it was Cassie.

Quickly, he crossed the street and ran after the woman and child.

"Cassie! Cassie!" he called.

The woman didn't turn.

Paul ran down the street after them. "Cassie! Cassie!"

Finally, he reached them.

"Cassie?"

The woman turned.

Paul recognized immediately the woman wasn't Cassie.

"What do you want?" she asked.

"Oh, sorry!" Paul said. "I thought you were someone else."

Annoyed, the woman turned quickly and continued up the street with the child.

Paul peered after the woman. *What's happening to me?* he thought. He would have sworn the woman was Cassie and the child was Paulie. Shaking his head with confusion and indecision, he walked back across the street to his truck.

* * * *

That night, he drove back to Knoxville. Upon arrival, his first thought was to go to the motel bar and get drunk, but he resisted the urge. He wanted his head clear for tomorrow. He was going to put all of his available energies and thoughts into his work.

At work the following morning, Will was there to greet him.

"You feeling better?"

Paul nodded.

"You look better," he said. "Okay. Get back out there. I'm looking for the old Paul on that motor grader today."

"Thanks for the understanding," Paul said.

Will peered at him for a moment. "Sorry if I was too hard on you last week," Will said. "You know my neck is on the line when one of my men does something like that."

"I know," Paul said. "You were just doing your job."

Over the next three weeks, Paul paid close attention to every detail of his work. Every time he would start a cut, he would get off the motor grader and check the exact markings on the stake. For all the previous years, he had not done that. These were critical times, he told himself. He couldn't afford another mistake like the last one. He had to be very careful.

Christmas 1964

For the 1964 Gartman Christmas party, Will had rented the reception room at the motel where the crew was living. As always, it was a festive affair with plenty of food and drink. The company had had a good year. Weather had been good, there were few breakdowns, and the Knoxville project was almost three months ahead of schedule. As a result of this success, the company was quite generous with its employees. Paul had received a five-hundred-dollar bonus, a pair of wool gloves, and a plaque denoting his long-time service to the company. As always at the finale of the festivities, the crew honored Will with a rousing rendition of "For He's a Jolly Good Fellow."

"For he's a jolly good fellow, for he's a jolly fellow," the crew sang, "For he's a jolly good fellow, which nobody can deny."

After the song ended, there was loud applause and partygoers prepared to leave. Outside, as Paul was going to his truck, Will called him aside.

"Can we talk for a minute?"

"Sure," Paul said.

Will was tweaking his mustache. "You heading down to Florida to see your dad?"

Paul nodded.

"Going to stop by Duck Springs?"

"Probably."

His foreman peered at him. "I hope you know what you're doing," Will said.

"I'm in too deep to get out now," Paul said.

"I was afraid of that," Will said.

A long pause.

"Remember what happened after your mother died?"

"I remember," Paul said. "And I'll always appreciate you for that."

Will didn't answer right away. "Next time, I might not be there."

"I have to take my chances," Paul said.

For a long moment, he peered at Paul. "You're on the edge of a cliff," he said. "The only thing between you and the bottom of that cliff is an old man trying to be a father to the son he never had."

Paul took a deep breath. "Right or wrong, I have to do it," Paul said.

"I understand," Will said. "A man's got to do what he's got to do." His face softened into a smile. "Okay," he said, offering his hand. "Merry Christmas and have a good trip to Florida."

"Merry Christmas to you," Paul said, shaking Will's hand.

Will turned toward his truck as Paul watched. Suddenly, Will turned.

"One more thing," Will said.

"What's that?"

"That little incident earlier this month about the cuts on the shoulder...."

"Yeah?"

"Nobody knows about that but me and you," Will said. "There's nothing on paper."

Paul smiled.

"Thanks!!" he said. "Merry Christmas!"

That night, when he returned to his room, Paul undressed and went straight to bed. He was already packed and he wanted to get a good night's rest and for his trip the following morning. After he drifted off to sleep, he dreamed he was with Cassie and their son and they were frolicking in an open, grassy field. Paul would playfully chase the baby and, as Cassie watched happily, the child squealed with delight. Each holding the child's hand, they swung the child between them; on a park bench, Paul held the baby in his lap and played patti-cake as the child giggled with delight; he and Cassie held the child between them in an embrace and kissed happily; the three of them were a happy family together.

* * * *

The following morning, Paul was up early and en route to his father's house. As he cruised south through north Georgia, he couldn't wait to see the homestead and refresh his memories. He wondered why Cassie hadn't written in over six months. He wondered if she was sick or too busy to write. There had to be some problem, he thought, or she would have contacted him. He thought he might get some clues at the homestead. Also, he was excited at the possibility of seeing his son again.

Just before noon, he turned off the main highway and headed toward Duck Springs. Once he rounded the curve, he drove past the homestead, turned around, and parked at the west end of the bridge. There, he took up a vigil. He reminded himself that, if Cassie saw his new truck, she wouldn't recognize it. After almost three years, the newness of the highway had disappeared. All of the vegetation destroyed by construction had regrown. Motorists had thrown empty cans and paper trash along the shoulders. "Donna loves Harold" had been spray-painted on the railing along the east end of the bridge. As he waited inside the truck, he rolled down the window. It was unseasonably warm for late December. Temperatures were in the high sixties and, somewhere, he could hear birds singing.

Not a lot had changed at the homestead. The peach trees were much larger now and instead of having posts for two rows of pole beans, there were now four. The young calf that had dragged her three years earlier was a young heifer and grazing quietly in the back pasture. A fresh washing was on the line. There were overalls, dresses, and clothes for a young toddler. The big rig and the old red pickup were in the front yard. Suddenly, he saw Cassie step off the back porch and start across the yard. Moments later, she entered the barn, strode through the hallway, and moved the heifer to the front pasture. Then he watched as she went to the far peach tree for a moment, then return to the house. That was the old signal she had used three years ago to notify him of their secret meetings. He wondered what she was doing. Who was she leaving a message for? He waited.

Ten minutes later, Cassie, her husband, and the two children came out of the house and got into the old red pickup. Paul watched curiously as the old truck bounced along the dirt road, then pulled out on the main highway toward Duck Springs. He waited. Suddenly, among the trees, he saw the figure of a man moving quickly along the river trail toward the cane break. What was happening? Had she broken her promise? Did she have a new lover? He was going to find out.

Quickly, he got out of the truck, stumbled down the embankment, and started running along the river trail. At the cane break, he stopped. Ahead of him, beyond the broomsage patch, he could see the man moving toward the peach tree. Moments later, he was in the barn hallway. He stopped and listened. No sound. Then he started for the peach tree.

As he approached, he could see the man standing under the peach tree and reaching for the fruit jar. For a moment, he stopped and stared. Then he rushed forward.

"Hey!" Paul called.

Startled, the man looked up.

"What are you doing?" Paul shouted.

"What are YOU doing?" the other man asked.

For a moment, the two glared at one another. Then Paul stepped forward.

"Give me that!" he said, snatching the fruit jar from the other man's hand.

For a moment, the other man stepped back. There was genuine fear in his eyes. "I don't want any trouble," the man said.

They glared at one another.

"Who are you?" the other man asked.

"None of your business," Paul said. "If you're smart, you'll get the hell out of here."

Instantly, at Paul's words, the other man turned and darted off down the path through the broomsage toward the river.

Paul opened the fruit jar and withdrew the note. It was Cassie's handwriting.

In the hay room tomorrow night. 8:30. Will have food.

He looked up from the note, trying to make sense of it. Suddenly, his mind was afire with anger and confusion. The note was meant for the other man! The woman who had promised her undying love had taken a new lover! His Annabel Lee was doing the same thing with another man that she had been doing with him. And using all of the same methodologies. Suddenly, the same sense of agonizing loss he had felt at his mother's death came flooding back into his consciousness. He peered toward the farmhouse. The very sight filled him with hatred and betrayal. So this was the meaning of life? This was the justice and peace and hope that life offers? He felt his sensibilities starting to crumble. He peered toward the highway and his truck. It was a vague blur. His thoughts came in fragments. His emotions were unravelling. He fell to his knees and, for a long moment, sobbed uncontrollably. Then, suddenly, he stood up. Now he could clearly see his truck again. He desperately wanted to hurt somebody or kill something for the agonizing rage he felt inside. He turned and raced back along the path to his truck. Once inside, he slammed the door, opened the glove compartment, and took out the pistol.

* * * *

Five minutes later, the old red pickup came slowly back around the curve. As the driver approached the bridge, he saw a late model pickup parked at the north end, its horn blaring without interruption. The old red pickup slowed and, as it passed the late model pickup, the driver glimpsed inside. Inside, he saw a lone man slumped over the steering wheel.

Curiously, he pulled the red pickup to the shoulder, then got out to inspect the scene. As he approached the truck, he could see the horn was blaring because the driver's dead body was slumped over the steering wheel. He peered inside. Blood from a head wound was running down the side of the man's face and onto the steering wheel, then dripping on the truck floorboard.

"My God!" he said.

Suddenly, behind him, his wife appeared, a small child at her side.

"Cassie, you shouldn't have that baby out here," the husband said. "He'll catch his death of cold. Get back in the truck with Timmy!"

Peering curiously at the truck, the woman didn't budge.

"I want to see what happened!" she replied.

Miffed, the man could see it was useless to press the issue.

"Some man shot hisself," he said finally.

"I want to see," she said.

She stepped forward and peered inside the pickup. For a moment, she stood frozen by what she saw.

"Oh, my God! Oh my God!" she screamed.

She released the child's hand and took out a handkerchief. Then, her face buried in the handkerchief, she sobbed uncontrollably. Then, apparently because the mother was crying, the child broke into a screaming wail.

The man looked at the woman with a puzzled look.

"Cassie, what's wrong with you?" he asked. "Why are you taking on like that? Do you know this man?"

The woman was trying to regain her composure. Finally, she wiped her eyes.

"No! I don't know him," she lied. "I cry when I see dead people. You know the way I am at funerals."

For a long moment, the man stared curiously at the woman, searching her face for an answer. There was none. Finally, he shook his head as if any further efforts would be futile.

He turned his attention to the screaming child.

"Paulie! Paulie! It's okay, baby," he said. "Stop crying, baby! Daddy is here. Everything will be okay."

The man picked up the child and held his head to his shoulder.

"Hush up, Paulie! Hush up, baby," the man said again, softly patting the baby's back. "Daddy is here. Daddy loves you. Everything will be fine."

The child was inconsolable.

Holding the screaming child in his arms, the man turned to the woman.

"Come on. Let's go to the house," he said. "I'll call the county."

Moments later, the woman, the man, and the screaming child were back in the old red pickup. The engine roared to life and it pulled off the road shoulder on to the highway. As it disappeared down the highway, the loud screaming of the child faded slowly away.

A Winter Afternoon II

A million times, I've remembered that horrible day. Seeing Paul's body slumped over the steering wheel of that pickup truck and the horn blaring like there was no tomorrow will live in my mind until the day I die. And every time I remember it, I search my heart and soul trying to discover what I could have done differently. And each and every time, I don't find an answer. All I can say is that he loved me too much. Although I loved him with all my heart, my life had to go on.

After I saw what happened to Paul, I ended the relationship with DeWayne. I knew I could never again go through with another man what I went through with Paul. Once was enough. I had enough guilt to last a lifetime. So I spent the next twenty-two years with Austin, living year after year in a passionless marriage. On one hand, I had this terrible need in my loins, but, on the other, I was too afraid to give in to it again. After a while, I stopped paying attention to it. It didn't go away. I just learned to live with it.

Timmy died in 1974. He lived until the age of twenty-two. That was two years longer than doctors had predicted. Four days after his nineteenth birthday, he went into fits while I was in Duck Springs paying the water bill. I had never seen him having fits like that. I didn't understand why because he had been taking his medicine. The woman behind the counter called an ambulance and they took Timmy to the hospital. For almost three weeks, he was in a coma and finally, the doctors said he should be sent to the state home in Valdosta. At the home, he got worse and worse. I don't believe the doctors really knew what to do, so they just gave him more and more medicine. It didn't seem to help. From time to time, me and Austin would go visit him, but he didn't recognize us. He didn't even know we were in the world. Part of me was relieved when he passed. I had seen him suffer for so long, I was just glad to see an end to it. It's a terrible thing to watch your child die a little each and every day. I hope God has a special place somewhere for Timmy.

In 1988, the end came for Austin while he was on a trip to the west coast, hauling air conditioners. He had spent the night at a truck stop in Burlingame, California and, during breakfast the next morning, he fell dead of a heart attack. He was fifty-eight. After all those years of just sitting in that truck cab, his weight got out of control. The doctors warned him, but he wouldn't exercise and never bothered to control his eating. I hated it, but there was nothing I could do.

After he died, I got a check from the trucking company for almost sixty thousand dollars. With that money, I put Paulie through college. After high school, he went up to Atlanta and got a degree in electrical engineering from Georgia Tech. He's fifty-three now. He works for the light company over in Albany and he and his wife Molly have given me three beautiful grandchildren. It's safe to say he has made his mama very proud.

Austin always believed Paulie was his child. He loved Paulie with all of his heart, but he never knew the truth. Some days, I think I might tell Paulie the truth. On other days, I think I might not. After all these years, I'm not sure there is anything to be gained. Sometimes, it's best to let sleeping dogs lie.

Now, in the west, I can see just a tiny piece of sun peeping over the treetops. The ducks are all gone and the sack of bread is empty. Along the sidewalk leading to the main building, I see Paulie coming to get me. He's wearing a jacket this time.

"How'd it go, Mama?"

"Oh, just fine."

"You ready to go in?"

"I'm ready."

* * * *

The son grasped the handles of the wheelchair and carefully maneuvered it across the brown grass, then onto the sidewalk.

"Did you have fun feeding the ducks?"

"Oh, yes," the mother replied. "I had a good long talk with myself."

"I'm glad," the son said.

For several minutes, the son pushed the wheelchair along the winter sidewalk without speaking. Finally, he spoke.

"I love you, Mama," he said.

"I love you too, baby," the mother replied.

* * * *

Wise men talk about the folly of youth. About how young people will take chances and do things they would never dare as older, wiser people. Whatever reason I had for doing what I did more than fifty years ago doesn't matter anymore. A life was lost, but a life was gained. It's all in the past now and neither me nor anyone else on this earth can change it. What's done is done. When I draw my last breath and the great darkness comes to surround me, I'll know one thing for sure. The only man I ever truly loved was Paul Hamilton. Although I knew we could never be together, I took what I could get while I could get it. If that's wrong, then so be it. Paul gave me the greatest joys I had ever known as a woman. Not only in the wonderful days we spent together, but in the gift of my son. In Paulie, I got what I wanted most, a normal, healthy child that I could love and be proud of and watch grow up to be somebody. I don't have enough words to say how much that means to me. Best of all, through my son, I will always have his father. Nobody, absolutely nobody, can ever take that away from me.

****The End****